FIND PECOS JOE

'Pecos Joe' Ralston was the only man who could prove Bill Stride's imprisoned brother Orville had been far away from Durango the day the bank was robbed. So, Bill swore to find him.

Ralston had been last heard of in Pan Town, Wyoming, and Bill Stride went there. He wasn't in the place long before he realised that 'Pecos Joe' was a sensitive subject – so sensitive, indeed, that he had to fight the bully, Dan Wall, with his fists, and then almost got himself poisoned.

What was the mystery surrounding this man, the nobody that it seemed everybody did not want found? There was gold in it, of course, and Stride needed all his wits to reach that last gun battle on the Powder River and the final ironies of a quest that need not have been.

By the same author

The Secret of Lost Butte

Find Pecos Joe

by

JACK GREER

A Black Horse Western

ROBERT HALE . LONDON

First published in Great Britain 1988

ISBN 0 7090 3395 8

Robert Hale Limited
Clerkenwell House
Clerkenwell Green
London EC1R OHT

Printed in Great Britain by
WBC Print Limited, Barton Manor, Bristol.
Bound by WBC Bookbinders Limited.

ONE

Bill Stride rode his horse slowly through the mud at the middle of the street. He had found it at last. This was Pan Town, Wyoming. Legends that confirmed it jutted from the fronts of the stores and other business properties along either side of the way. Though this could be regarded as little more than the beginning, he felt a certain relief, for a man could get himself lost in the Powder River country about as effectively as anywhere on earth, and he had been lost once or twice just lately.

The wind drove some more of the thin, cold rain that had been falling all day into his face. Stride shivered under his heavy serge jacket. This was mid-April – Spring – but the weather didn't seem to have heard about it, and was behaving like mid-February. But it was no good complaining, by word or thought. Bad though the day might be, it was the only one around, and about as good as any other for the start of what he had to do.

He turned his black gelding towards a hitching rail on his right. Then he swung down, sinking ankle-deep into the mire, and sloshed around a bit while securing his mount. After that, wet of backside and very stiff, he eased his spine and looked up at the rain glistening on the newly varnished timbers of Jake's Palace, Saloon and Gambling House, reflecting that, just as the day was about as good as any other for the beginning of this business, so this establishment was about as good as any other to enter and start asking questions. Indeed, it might prove a great deal better, since saloon company was at its most plentiful in bad weather and men who drank much whisky were usually the most ready of tongue.

Of course it had really commenced when Bill Stride had visited his brother Orville in Denver Prison a few weeks ago. 'Find "Pecos Joe" Ralston', Orv had begged. 'He was in Pan Town, Wyoming, accordin' to his last letter. Ask him to testify to the Authorities that him and me was fishin' at Blue Mesa lake on the day that the Columbia and South Colorado Bank was robbed in Durango'. Thus had Orville Stride spoken, and now Bill was about to follow up his brother's entreaty – which, on the face of it, should be easy, but "Pecos Joe" Ralston was cursed with a fiddlefoot and might be almost anywhere within a few hundred miles by this time. In fact finding him could prove the work of months or even a virtual impossibility.

The verandah at the front of Jake's Palace was served by three wooden steps. On the right of the steps, and at their foot, was an iron scraper. Stride went to the scraper and removed some of the mud that he had just picked up on his riding boots. Then he gave himself a couple of hard shakes to get rid of some of the water that clung to his top garments, and climbed next to the saloon's main entrance, parting the batwings and entering a new and shiny bar. His ears were at once assailed by roaring talk and tinny music, his nostrils by the reek of alcohol, tobacco, and drying clothes, and his eyes by the semi-drunken motley which kept up a slow, unconscious dance about the floor which was threaded by the grinning death masks of the white limbed whores who ambled their predatory rounds with the affectation of a whisking fan or a tea cup jiggling on a china saucer. This, Stride decided at first glance, was a rich community – new rich, maybe – but rich and determined to enjoy it, and he realized that the mines lately opened up along the nearby Powder River must be yielding fortunes on the evidence of this open-handed and uninhibited scene.

Stride pushed his way up to the long bar. There were three people serving. Two were male, overweight, florid, bald and sweating, and the third was a bold-eyed, brassy blonde of about thirty-five. She had the now slightly sagging body of a woman who had known what it was all about, and she turned away from a less pleasing customer to put herself before Stride's lean and handsome six-feet three-inches the instant that she cottoned to his presence. 'Hi, feller,' she greeted. 'New in town?'

'That's it,' Stride agreed, catching a glimpse of his frank-eyed and straight-nosed face in the backbar mirror. 'Just got here. It's a foul day outside.'

'It surely is,' the barmaid agreed. 'What's it to be?'

'Beer, please.'

'A man with manners,' the woman observed, half-mocking and half-appreciative as she lifted down a glass and then started filling it from a cask of light beer that was chocked up on her left. 'Don't often hear a "please" in here. Have to feed the hogs for that.'

Stride laughed obligingly. 'Mind if I ask a question, miss?'

'It gets better,' the blonde said archly. 'On such a short acquaintance too.' Her blue eyes slanted at him quizzically. 'Depends of what it is,' she added more seriously. 'Pan Town is like any other. There are some questions you can ask, and others it's better not to.'

'Asking after a man, that's all.'

Nodding, she set his beer down in front of him, and he paid her with a silver dollar. She held the coin between finger and thumb and stood there, waiting.

'Does the name "Pecos Joe" Ralston mean anything to you?'

'Sure. I knew "Pecos Joe". Most everybody did.'

'Did?'

'He isn't around any more.'

'As of when?'

'Not for a month.'

'Any idea where he went?'

The blonde shook her head. Then one of the barmen leaned over and gave her a poke in the ribs. 'On vacation, Hetty?' he gravelled. 'Earn your keep, woman!'

'The day you don't drink yours up, Ken!' Hetty

snapped in reply. 'Sling your hook!'

The barman moved away, muttering to himself.

'Gandy Burridge is your man,' Hetty said, pointing quickly across the bar at a yawning, matchstick figure, with a thin, hooked nose, bulging eyes behind steel-rimmed glasses, and an air of dribbling vacuity. 'Gandy knows all that goes on in town. Take him a beer, and ask him what you've asked me.'

Nodding, Stride began digging for another coin.

'I've got enough here,' the barmaid advised, tossing the silver dollar which she still held between finger and thumb into one of the money pots of the backbar and then stepping aside to fill another glass with beer.

'The guy looks a bit dopey to me,' Stride observed, as the blonde placed the second measure of beer beside the first.

'Don't let his looks deceive you,' Hetty responded. 'That's a wise old bird. Take my word for it.'

'I will.'

'Off you go.'

Stride spoke his thanks. Then, with a glass in either hand, he turned away from the bar and slowly zigged and zagged a course across the densely populated floor, arriving at the spot by the side wall where Gandy Burridge sat with no drop of beer spilled and a disarming smile on his face. 'Will you have a beer with me, sir?' he asked.

Burridge considered him for a long moment with eyes that looked far less the idiot's than they had from the distance. 'What is it you want?' he asked. 'I saw you talking to Hetty Gage. Did she send you over?'

'As a matter-of-fact she did.'

Burridge extended his right hand towards the glass of beer in Stride's left, giving a chair opposite him a kick from beneath the table at which he sat. Stride let Burridge's fingers close on the glass, then pulled out a chair on Gandy's immediate right and sat down. 'I believe "Pecos Joe" Ralston has left town. Can you say where he's gone?'

'No.'

'No, you don't know?' Stride asked, faintly annoyed by the uncaring bluntness of the other's reply. 'Or – no, you won't tell me?'

'No, I don't know.'

Stride gazed at Burridge fixedly. He felt intuitively that this strange caricature of a man was not telling the truth. 'I was told you know everything that happens in Pan Town.'

'Hetty Gage exaggerates,' Burridge said acidly. 'She's the one with all the know. There's no worse gossip in Wyoming than Hetty.'

'She struck me as being rather cautious,' Stride observed.

'She once caught a nasty hiding off her boss,' Burridge returned with some relish. 'She was Jake Pelman's top whore that time o' day, and got into the habit of talkin' too much of his business while she was between the blankets. Jake removed her from what y'might call close contact with his customers after that. That's how she comes to be behind the bar – and sendin' you over to me.'

'History,' Stride commented, presuming Jake

Pelman to be the owner of the Palace. 'I'm interested in more recent events. Even the smallest hint would be a help.'

'Can see,' Burridge acknowledged, a goggle eye now showing grey and crafty through the lense that covered it. 'What's so important about "Pecos Joe"? Ralston was nobody special time he was about here.'

'I've never met "Pecos Joe" Ralston,' Stride admitted, 'and I know as little about him as I know about you and Hetty Gage. But "Pecos Joe" can swear out evidence that should free a man who'll otherwise rot in the jail for the next fifteen years.'

'Who?'

'Orville Stride, my brother. That's why I'm pressing more than's polite.'

'I still don't know a thing,' Burridge said with a finality that contained overtones of dislike.

Stride lifted his palms and let them fall on the sodden cloth that covered his thighs. 'If you don't, you don't. Okay, Mr Burridge. But can you point out anybody in this room who might be able to help me?'

'No.'

'Can you name anybody in the town?'

'No.'

'Then,' Stride sighed, 'I shall just have to start asking around as best I can.'

'I wouldn't do that,' Burridge cautioned.

'Why not?'

'There are folk around who don't cotton to strangers who ask questions.'

'About "Pecos Joe"?'

'About him,' Burridge agreed, the threatening note in his voice quite open now – 'about anybody. You brought me a drink, and I'm going to return kindness for kindness. Leave town. Right now. Go elsewhere and ask your questions.'

'Isn't that the point?' Stride wondered. 'I'll be happy to go elsewhere and ask my questions – if you or somebody will suggest where. I was given Pan Town as a starting point, and what's the sense of a starting point if you don't start there.'

'Mister, you're a sight too persistent for your own good,' Burridge said coldly. 'You're fast runnin' out of luck. I've done with you.'

Stride gave the other a curt little nod. He rose to his feet, beer glass once more in hand, and turned away from Burridge's table. Then he threaded a path across the room and halted now at the end of the long bar furthest from the street. Here he backed himself into the corner formed by wall and divide and began shooting glances that both sought and calculated among the people present. He was looking for some person who gave the impression of being at once approachable and an established citizen, but it was hard to detect anybody who bore the unmistakable marks – if indeed they existed outside his imagination – and then his mind was faintly troubled by the fact that Gandy Burridge had left his table and walked to a door that gave access to a back room, where he had begun talking with a hard-faced, fiery-looking young man of a height and other physical characteristics that matched Stride's own. As the talk developed, the big fellow started slanting dagger-sharp looks in the watcher's direction, and there was soon no doubt in Stride's mind that he was the subject of the conversation between Burridge and the big man.

Stride took a pull at his beer. He went on gazing about him as before, and letting the moments drift. He had strong intimations of trouble in the offing, and knew that he ought to walk out of the saloon at once. These little thrills of warning intensified as Burridge and the big guy parted, the former returning to his table and the latter folding his arms and lounging against the jamb of the doorway that he occupied. The big man shut his eyes, and seemed to have lost interest in everything; but Stride knew that the other was watching him still through slightly parted lids and just waiting for him to either accost somebody else or show signs of so doing.

The sense of intimidation rested on Stride's brain like a physical presence. It provoked and aggravated, goading him to run, and slowly bringing out the best – or worst – in a defiant nature that would not be bullied or pushed around. Suddenly Stride could stand it no longer, and knew that the thing must be put to the test. Thus, spotting a large, bearded man who was prominent among the onlookers at a poker table near the centre of the room, Stride placed his beer on the bar and then began making for the citizen whom he had singled out, moving deliberately enough to leave the big guy at the entrance to the back room no doubt as to his plan.

The indolent figure against the jamb came abruptly

to life. He advanced swiftly into the room, shoving aside drinkers en route, and placed himself between Stride and the bearded man, who obviously had no idea of what was happening in his vicinity. Then the tall fellow with the hard face put out a staying hand in Stride's direction and snapped: 'You get one chance! Get out!'

Stride halted, just short of the other's touch. 'One chance, eh? Tut, tut. Sounds frightening!'

'It had better be. You've been told.'

'Hold on,' Stride advised amiably. 'You the boss?'

'No.'

'Bouncer?'

'No.'

'Just Gandy's pal, eh? The twins – no-this and no-that.'

'My name is Dan Wall,' the big man said with all the arrogance of one who knew himself to be known.

'Dan Wall?' Stride mused. 'Dan Wall? I can see you expect your name to mean something to me. Sorry. It means nothing.'

'Think again, damn your eyes!'

'Shouldn't it be ears?' Stride inquired innocently, scratching his head. 'Wall? – Wall? – Wall?' He sighed regretfully; but then a great light seemed to burst upon him. 'Why, of course! There's a no-good pistolero of that name who's been bullying his way around the Northwest in recent years. But you're obviously not that Dan Wall. No, sir. You don't wear your gun right, and you look sort of leery rather than bad. Not up to the part at all!'

'Are you going?'

'No,' Stride replied, his voice losing its banter and his gaze hardening. 'I've got business in these parts, and I mean to exercise my right as a free man and stay.'

'You've sassed me something wicked,' Wall snarled, 'and now I'm going to break every bone in your body!'

'You can try,' Stride cautioned.

Wall stepped in, left fist rifling. The blow thudded into Stride's solar plexus, and ought to have dropped him, but he had been anticipating some such punch and tensed his belly muscles moments ago. Grinning, he absorbed the force of the shot without blinking and whipped over a right hook for which the gunman was totally unprepared. The blow took Wall on the side of the chin and dumped him on his backside.

The downed man just sat there for a moment, murderous of gaze and licking blood; and, as all the noise in the bar-room ceased and heads turned to find out what was happening, Stride said in his loudest voice: 'I've been asking after the whereabouts of "Pecos Joe" Ralston, and I'd be mighty obliged if there's anybody present who can be of help.'

Wall let out a wild yell. He sprang to his feet, then waded in with both fists swinging. Stride slipped a left hook, blocked a crossing right, ducked, weaved, and generally weathered the storm, buckling his opponent's nose with a straight left in the course of the action; but then his left heel caught an accidentally tripping foot that jutted from beneath a nearby table and he staggered into a big right that grazed his left temple and spun him round. Belly-first, he collapsed across the centrally placed poker table, and the legs of the table gave away under the weight and force of his arrival and he ended up on the floor amidst cards and showering blue chips.

A trifle dazed, he made an instant attempt to rise, but succeeded only in tipping into a sitting position similar to the one which Wall had occupied a few moments before. Shaking his head, he fought to recover his wits and full powers of movement, and was for that second at the mercy of the man who now towered above him. Dipping, Wall seized him by the lapels and jerked him to his feet; then, leaning back to give himself maximum leverage, the gunman prepared to strike for the jaw with a knock-out blow; but Stride fell deliberately inside the other's guard and clapped smothering palms on Wall's biceps, killing the finisher before it got started and checking at source such blows as he essayed next.

Moving to bellows of encouragement from around the bar, the two big men went into an ungainly waltz, and might have kept it up for half a minute; but then Stride put all his strength into a shove that sent Wall staggering to the rear. The gunman came into violent contact with the edge of the bar but, jarred though he was, remained upright and bounced back at his advancing foe, right fist hitting out straight from the shoulder. The blow detonated at the middle of Stride's forehead and stopped him in his tracks. Then Wall kicked the legs from under him and he fell onto his back. In almost the same instant, Stride glimpsed his opponent diving at him, with the clear intention of pinning him to the floor, but he managed to get his knees up and caught the other in mid-flight, toppling him aside.

They struggled to their feet, one hardly less winded than the other, but both determined and, all science now lost, they waded in, battering away at head and body with all their force, and both had taken a lot of punishment, when Wall suddenly crossed with a left that once more fetched up Stride in his tracks; but the gunman's face showed that, despite his success, he no longer trusted his punch, and he put down his left shoulder and charged. Stride took the full force of Wall's arrival in the middle of his chest, and the charge sent him flying. He landed on the floorboards a moment later with a crash that made the whole room shudder. Wall bounded at him now, kicking. Rolling this way and that, Stride protected his vitals as best he could – and did a fairly good job of it – but nevertheless collected a number of deep bruises on the belly and thighs before Wall, frustrated, stepped in close, obviously to have a go at the groin, and gave his opponent the chance that he had been praying for.

Shooting his legs out straight, Stride sat up abruptly and, locking his arms around Wall's knees, threw himself onto his back again and heaved, pitching the gunman through the air like a tossed balk of timber. Wall hit the floor several yards beyond the point from which he had started out and, hands arrowing, cut through a number of tables and chairs, glass smashing and other wreckage raining down as the crown of his head drove into the partition on the right of the main exit and brought him to a stop.

Stride dragged himself to his feet. Favouring the contused state of his lower body, he limped towards the felled gunman – intending to heave him off the floor and hit him just once more – but Wall surprised him by getting up and facing round again, fight still apparent in his bearing. Enraged by Wall's sheer durability, Stride made the charge his own this time. He wrapped his arms around the gunman's hips, and the impetus of his movement carried them both through the batwings and out onto the verandah. Here, at the head of the steps that gave access to the main, they punched and wrestled briefly, then rolled down the flight and ended in the mire of the street below.

Spitting and spluttering, they broke apart, crouching on hands and knees and glowering at each other. Stride felt suddenly awful, punched out and sick at the belly. He knew he'd got to finish this quickly or suffer the consequences, and he thought about this for a second too long, failing to see Wall's hands reaching for his throat until it was almost too late.

Instinctively, he struck upwards with both fists, catching the insides of the gunman's wrists with his knuckles and knocking Wall's hands aside. Then he hooked with left and right, both punches finding the point of his opponent's chin, and Wall's skull snapped back hard on his spine, the momentary pressure on his spinal cord paralysing him and leaving him wide-eyed and kneeling. Rising then, the mud running black off his fingertips, Stride drove punches into the face turned up at him. The blows flattened Wall, and he sank into the surface of the street; and it was only when an onlooker's shout reminded that the gunman was in danger of drowning that Stride halted his battering fists.

Now, seeing that there was no longer any movement in his adversary, Stride reached down through the mud and pulled Wall's head and shoulders back into the air. Then he seized the other by the collar and dragged him to the nearest horse trough, picking him up from the waist and dumping him into the water. Wall recovered his senses at the first touch of the cold liquid, and sat there a moment or two threshing and spitting; then he swung his legs clumsily over the edge of the tank and slid back to an erect position, moving his hand in the direction of his gun; but Stride stepped in promptly and robbed him of his weapon, throwing it into the horse trough which its owner had just vacated. After that he stepped back, setting his arms akimbo, and waited to see what Wall would do next.

The gunman shook a fist, but was clearly beaten, and he turned away and went slogging up street through the mud towards a big black horse that stood at the last of the hitching rails which served Jake's Palace. Then, freeing the brute, he speared a stirrup and dragged himself into his saddle, doubling forward exhaustedly before peering round his left shoulder and displaying his much battered face as he said: 'We'll finish this another time.'

'I thought we had finished it,' Stride returned. 'You

look all finished to me.'

'No, no,' Wall responded. 'Draw-and-shoot. We'll finish it permanently.'

'If that's what you want,' Stride said.

'Stick around.'

'Just maybe, Wall,' Stride temporised. 'I've got better things to do than wait around to show great men how little they really are.'

'I'll find you!' Wall declared, kicking his horse into motion and heading slowly northwards.

'I'll look forward to it,' Stride promised, grinning a lopsided grin for the benefit of the watchers. But, inwardly, he was much less sure of himself; for, though he knew he had Wall's measure with his fists, he wished the talk of guns had not come up. When it came to shooting, you could never be sure how the thing would turn out.

TWO

After acknowledging a few congratulations on the thrashing he had just given a man 'badly in need of one', Stride walked his horse along to the Tonsorial, had a bath and general clean up, then put on a change of garments from his gunny sack and made inquiries of the barber as to where rooms were to be rented in town. He was given three addresses, but assured that Sadie Aitken's boarding house – 'just down the road and a door or two short of Bright's livery stables' – was the best; so, on leaving the Tonsorial and once more heading north, he called in at Sadie Aitken's place and booked himself a room. This was number twelve, on the top floor, and it suited him very nicely. Thus, with his bed assured and the promise of a fire to sit over, he led his mount along to the livery stables and saw to its needs before taking himself into Cooper's saloon – a spit-and-sawdust establishment across the main street from Bright's – and buying himself a bottle of Red Chief, *the* rye whisky, guaranteed to remove the edge from any suffering and cure most ills.

Bottle in pocket, he returned to Sadie Aitken's

boarding house and went up to his room, where a coal fire was now blazing in the grate and a chair had been put in place for him on the hearth rug. Confessing to himself that he was currently a wreck and hadn't felt worse since he had the chickenpox all of fifteen years ago, he lowered himself gingerly into the chair and removed the Red Chief from his coat, pulling the cork with a bruised hand and then putting the bottle to his mouth and pouring a fair quantity of the ninety-six proof spirit down his throat. Then, re-corking the bottle, he set it down on the right-hand side of his chair – against the probable need of another pull in a few minutes time – and closed his eyes, the alcohol soon filling him with a hazy warmth and making the world seem a slightly better place for hard-pressed cowhands and small dogs.

By heck! What was he to make of it? And him a peace-loving guy – until somebody went and put him out anyhow. One thing was dead certain. There were folk in this town who didn't want questions asked about "Pecos Joe" Ralston. Now why would that be? Obviously because the folk in question didn't want him located. Living – or dead? Yes, it could be that somebody had murdered the man and given him a secret grave. But why would anybody want to slay a guy who was probably little better than a saddle-tramp? And what could such a man know – if living – that others were prepared to ensure he was not put in the position to impart? It had to be something pretty big, and less than legal. But, whatever it was, Stride really didn't give a damn. Sure, he had his respect for the law, but all he wanted in the present circumstances was a sworn statement from "Pecos Joe" to the effect that he and Orville Stride had been fishing at Blue Mesa lake on the day that the Columbia and South Colorado Bank had been robbed at Durango. If he could get that, Dan Wall, Gandy Burridge, and whomsoever, could do what they liked, be it ne'er so illegal, and he wouldn't be even the smallest bit interested. Let them have their crazy dreams, and he would keep his small ambitions. If he could get brother Orv out of jail, he would be satisfied for this year. Hell! He could see for himself that his purpose was good and his motives right. So why had everything started to go wrong? He only wanted to help an innocent man, and was perfectly prepared to spend his savings from work on the range to that end. It made a man wonder why the Good Lord didn't show more plainly that He was on the side of the innocent.

Reaching down with his right hand, Stride was about to pick up his bottle of Red Chief again, when a knock sounded at the door and caused him to stay his movement. 'Who is it?' he called.

There was no answer. Frowning, he jacked himself erect and drew his Colt; then, turning from his chair, he began a silent advance in the direction of the door – side-stepping to his left across the face of the woodwork and shouldering up to the wall on that hand. Now, cocking the pistol, he quickly opened his door and thrust the weapon into the gap – much to the consternation of the tall and darkly pretty young woman who stood in the corridor outside, the fur collar of her unbuttoned coat clasped tightly about her throat and somehow placing too much emphasis on the heavily made up state of her features. 'Oops!' Stride confessed, grinning rather shamefacedly as he shut down the hammer of his gun and restored the Colt to its holster. 'Sorry, miss. I'm a mite jumpy. Had me an afternoon, as they say.'

'I know,' the girl answered, her voice low and holding a note of sympathy. 'I was there. You didn't see me, but I saw you.'

'Jake's Palace?'

She nodded. 'I work there. You're man enough to know what doing.'

'And not to say,' he agreed. 'What – ?'

'Aren't you going to invite me in?'

He opened the door wide. The girl stepped into the room. She paused momentarily in the grey light from the window, then walked over to the fire and held out her hands to the dancing flames. 'What a day,' she murmured; and the rain outside lashed the window-panes, as if to make her point.

'Spring,' Stride agreed disdainfully, moving up to stand on the opposite side of the hearth. 'Well – what do you want?'

'Your name is Stride, isn't it?'

'Yes – Bill.'

'I'm Sandra Aves,' she said, 'and I heard what you asked about "Pecos Joe" Ralston.'

'You did?' He patted the chair from which he had himself arisen. 'Have a seat.'

She sat down. 'I'm glad you gave Dan Wall snuff.

He's a bad man, and he's been asking for it.'

'So others have said.'

'Are you good with a gun?'

'Middling.'

'Wall is lightning fast, but he doesn't always shoot straight. There's your chance. Keep the range long, and you'll match him.'

'I'd rather not try,' Stride admitted, 'but I've got the feeling I'll have to. That's for another day. What about "Pecos Joe"? What can you tell me concerning him, Miss Aves? Do you have any idea where he's gone?'

'I saw him yesterday,' she replied, 'and it wasn't very far away.'

'Where? How far?'

'In the woods, close to Powder River, not five miles west of here.'

'That's fine,' Stride said. 'What was he doing?'

'Doing?'

'Panning? Digging? Hunting, maybe?'

'No,' the girl said. 'I was out riding – something I do when I get the chance – and I happened to see him through the trees. I believe he was collecting firewood.'

'Sounds like he's camping out there,' Stride commented. 'When was he last in town?'

'It must be a month ago.'

'That would square with the information I was given,' Stride mused, forehead gathering as he calculated. 'But take that month away and he must have lived in Pan Town some while.'

'Three months,' Sandra Aves responded. 'Mostly he worked around the saloons. As a cook or swamper; or sometimes behind the bar.'

'Unusual for him, as I understand it,' Stride growled. 'He's got a fiddlefoot and is constantly on the move. I wonder if his stay in Pan Town lasted so long because he was waiting for something?'

'For what?' the girl asked. 'Do people always have to behave exactly in character?'

'I don't know,' Stride admitted, unsure of what he was getting at himself. 'They usually do, that's all, and mostly have a strong reason when they don't.'

'Why is "Pecos Joe" – so important to you?' Sandra Aves inquired uncomfortably. 'I'm not nosey, but – '

'You'd like to know,' Stride said, shrugging. 'Well, it's no secret – and owing for your help, I reckon.' He went on to tell her of brother Orv's predicament, and of how "Pecos Joe" Ralston was the one man who could prove that Orville Stride had not been within a hundred miles of Durango on the day that the Columbia and South Colorado Bank had been robbed. 'It was just before Orv was sentenced at the end of last year,' he continued after a pause. 'He received a letter from Ralston that was forwarded to the prison from a hotel in Denver. In it "Pecos Joe" said that he was stopping awhile at Pan Town, in the Powder River district of Wyoming. I guess brother Orv could have written after Ralston's help, but he told me – when I visited him – that the man's notorious for his fiddlefoot and unreliable too. I reckon Orv figured that I'd be able to talk more aid out of the

Texan than his written words would get. Sort of speculating, I figure, too, Ralston is maybe no lover of the law.'

'Not from the company that he kept about here,' the girl remarked. 'So that's the story. I think it's just that your brother is a good judge. He knows that you're a persuasive man who'll do everything possible to see him freed.'

'I'll surely do all in my power to show "Pecos Joe" his duty to a friend,' Stride said a trifle grimly.

'You're certain your brother is innocent?' Sandra Aves queried. 'I'd hate to see a man like you made a monkey of.'

Stride smiled tolerantly. 'Natural to give it a thought, I guess. But I wouldn't be here if I wasn't sure about Orv. Oh, he's no saint, and I don't suppose he's lived honestly all the time, but he wasn't guilty of this one. He's the victim of mistaken identify or false witness. Fact is, the men who committed the robbery – four of them – have never been caught. Where you get a big crime, somebody – anybody, when it comes to keeping the book straight – has to pay. Orville's paying for that lot. He did no worse on the day the Columbia and South Colorado Bank was robbed than lift a few perch out of the lake.'

'It sounds like a bad miscarriage of justice,' the girl conceded. 'I'm sorry for any person who's been unjustly locked away. But, as it stands, I've done what I can here.'

'You'd do more if you could?' Strike asked swiftly.

'Why, yes,' she answered defensively, a startled

look in the eyes she turned up at him.

'You can do more.'

'How?'

'Got any time off tomorrow?'

'The only time I get off any day is what I lose from my sleep.'

'How's that, Miss Aves?'

'The girls at the Palace have to work until four a.m.,' she explained. 'The trade goes dead at about that time, and we're free to sleep. But we have to be up and start hustling again by noon.'

'Sounds like slavery.'

'Jake Pelman is the hardest boss in town. He'd fire me if he knew I'd come here.'

'That doesn't make me feel good about it,' Stride growled. 'I'm surprised you took such a chance over a question asked when the fists were flying. Oh, I'm glad you did; it was in a good cause, or so I deem it. But I smell a woman's curiosity too.'

'I suppose so,' she admitted. 'I can't altogether explain it. I felt somehow that I ought to come and find you; and – and I guess I was sort of interested in you as well.' There was a small shrug of the shoulders and a helpless gesture of the hands. 'Anyhow, I inquired as to what had become of you – Gandy Burridge had found out – then sneaked out of the back at the Palace and found my way up here.'

'We have it as is,' Stide commented. 'Can you spare some more sleep – to go riding with a man you're interested in?'

'You want me to show you where I saw "Pecos Joe"

Ralston,' the girl observed shrewdly.

'Yes, I do.'

'That's not very flattering,' she said wryly. 'But what else would it be for? I'm no better than I should be.'

'Neither am I, Miss Aves,' he chuckled. 'I'm the other half of the cathouse.'

'You said your name was Bill.'

He laughed. It was easy to like her. She had just demonstrated a quick wit and a ready sense of humour.

'Sandra.'

'Nice name. I'd said so before – in my head.'

A smile glimmered in her eyes, and passed. 'If we leave Pan Town at nine o'clock tomorrow morning, we ought to be able to get there and back by noon, without pushing ourselves unduly.'

'All I want you to do is show me the spot,' he said. 'You can leave me to it after that.'

'That's right,' she admitted. 'But I'll be curious. You will let me know how it comes out, Bill?'

'I'll come along and tell you,' he assured her, 'when I get the chance. And should it all work out as I hope, and they free brother Orv before too long, I'll send him here to say "thank you". You'll like that. He's a dab hand at pleasing the ladies, and better looking than I am.' He winced as he fingered a bruised cheek. 'Especially right now.'

'Handsome men,' the girl sighed. 'I've summered and I've wintered you, and there isn't one of you worth a wooden nickel. But you're all there is.' Rising from the chair, she walked slowly towards the door, looking back over her left shoulder. 'It's time I showed myself again at Jake's Palace. Tomorrow morning, then. Nine o'clock sharp, at the livery stables.'

'You keep your horse there?'

Nodding, she turned the knob and stepped out of the room, leaving the door open. Stride went to it and stood on the threshold, listening to her descent of the nearby stairs, her brief exchange of pleasantries with Mrs Aitken in the hall, and then the noise of her departure from the house through the front door. After that he closed up and ambled back to the chair before the fire, sitting down again and helping himself to another drink from his bottle of rye whisky. Then, his mind still full of Sandra Aves, he went over the important parts of his talk with her and once more posed the riddle of "Pecos Joe", questioning now why a man who had proved his ability to get a living in town should be roughing it beside the river. If Ralston had been waiting around the district for a planned event to occur – or the advent of somebody in particular – he could more easily have passed his time in Pan Town than camping in the wilds. But there was no accounting for tastes. His own ran to rye whisky just now, and he grinned a trifle dunkenly at the dubious comparison. The thing was to find "Pecos Joe", and he would do that tomorrow. For now, he would sleep and forget his hurts; and that was what he did.

THREE

He was awakened by another knock on the door, and slowly came to himself through the pulsing of his brain and the aching of his limbs. Yawning, he dully formed the notion that the rat-tat-tatting on the nearby woodwork had already been repeated several times and that he had been about as deeply asleep as a man could be. He opened his eyes into a room that was pitch dark except for a small red glow before him — the remains of the earlier blaze in the grate — and realized that night had fallen while he slept and his fire almost burned out.

Rising from his chair, full of sick shivers, Stride put a hand into a trouser-pocket and brought out a sulphur tip. Firing the match with his thumbnail, he turned upwards the flame thus produced and then faced into the room, peering through the light that flickered about him in search of the lamp.

The knocking at the door came again, downright insistent now. 'Hold on!' he called. 'Got to light a lamp in here. Can't find the damned thing!'

Once more the fist in the corridor hammered at the

woodwork. 'Hell!' Stride exploded. 'Who it is?'

'Jimmy Dankworth,' a boy's voice replied.

'Do I know you?'

'No, sir.'

'Didn't think I did,' Stride slurred, trying to shake himself fully awake and extinguishing his match in the process.

Swearing under his breath, he dug out and fired up another, deciding that he would waste no more time on locating the lamp for now. 'What is it, boy?' he demanded, shuffling in the direction of the door.

'You're wanted, Mr Stride.'

'Mr Stride, eh? Seems to me everybody knows my g'damned name!'

'Sir?' the boy's voice queried uneasily.

'Okay, okay,' Stride muttered half-apologetically, opening the door, and the light from the hanging-lamp that was burning under the ceiling of the passage outside showed him the pink and guileless face of a curly-haired twelve-year old with a freckled nose. 'Who wants me, Jimmy?'

'Mr Lambourne, sir.'

'Who's he when he's at home?' Stride asked.

'The manager of the bank.'

'The bank manager!' Stride exclaimed, blowing out what was laft of the second match as it threatened to burn his fingers and wondering at the same time just how much of the rye whisky he had consumed. 'Dammit, boy! I'm a stranger in town! I didn't get in until this afternoon – unless I'm Rip van Winkle. What business can the bank manager possibly have with me? Is he touting for accounts?'

'What's that?' the boy inquired vacuously.

'Skip it, son!' Stride advised. 'Where's this Mr Lambourne to be found?'

'At his house. I'm to take you there.'

'Is it far?'

'Nowhere's far in Pan Town, sir.'

'Ask a silly question,' Stride said, chiding himself, 'and rely on a kid to give you a sensible answer. Righto, Jimmy – lead on!'

The boy moved off to his left. Stride stepped out into the passage and shut the door of his room behind him. Then he followed the youngster, and they came to the landing and descended the stairs, entering the hall, with its frayed carpet underfoot, mirrors on either hand, and guardian hatrack and grandfather clock near the front door.

They passed between these sentinels and the boy opened the way into the night and they stepped directly onto the street, the boardwalk squelching under their weight. Now Jimmy Dankworth turned right and led southwards, the guttering brightness of the flares along the main street tossing their shadows with many another and bringing vivid islands of detail out of the drab backgrounds that climbed briefly on either side. Resting a hand on his guide's left shoulder, Stride walked onwards with care, thankful that the rain had almost ceased and that the wind was blowing less cold than it had during the day, and presently the boy stopped at a whitened step and knocked on the door behind it, his sigh of relief telling that his job was done.

The door opened. Lamplight streamed out of the house. Then a hand holding a quarter thrust into the radiance. Jimmy Dankworth took the coin, spoke his thanks, and faded into the gloom of the street beyond, feet splashing; while the door opened wide and a big, paunchy, square-shouldered man, with round eyes under a superior brow, manifested fully on the whitened step and said: 'Ah, Mr Stride. I'm Colley Lambourne. Thank you for coming along. Pray forgive this intrusion on your leisure, but I felt it necessary that we meet without further delay. Enter, please.'

Stride stepped indoors, more bewildered than ever, but passed no comment. The fat man faced about and led off down the hall. Stride pulled the front door shut, then made after him. The banker turned through the first door on the right, and Stride followed him into a large room that was lighted at four different points by brass oil-lamps with twin globes. The walls had been expensively papered, Turkey carpets lay on the floor, and the room was otherwise elegantly furnished with European pieces from the last century. The very atmosphere carried a feeling of taste and refinement that seemed totally out of place in this raw western town. Stride was impressed, despite himself, for he had already sensed that Lambourne was a hard man at root, though something of a poseur socially.

The banker led him to a spot before the marble fireplace where a table had been drawn up between facing chairs. On the table stood a cut-glass decanter and matching glasses into which generous measures of whisky had already been poured. A cigar box was also present, and its silver lid stood open to reveal the long green Cuban cigars within. Lambourne shepherded Stride to the chair on the further side of the table and gently sat him down. Then he said: 'Help yourself to a smoke. The whisky is already there.'

'Thank you,' Stride said, smiling his refusal of a cigar and retreating inwardly from his whisky glass, for the throbbing in his skull warned him that alcohol had already done him enough harm for one day. Then, wincing at the pain the movement cost him, he twisted his head and looked up at the bank manager. 'What is this, Mr Lambourne? What do you want with me? There can't be a previous connection – of any kind. I'm a cowhand, and my affairs are too limited.'

The banker moved to the second chair and seated himself. Picking up his glass, he saluted Stride with it, holding the gesture as he waited for its return. Lifting his own glass, Stride obliged, but did not drink, and he noticed that the other was irritated by this. Lambourne looked away momentarily, frowning, then brought his eyes back quickly to Stride's face and said: 'There is a previous connection. Or I think there may be.'

'Will you explain that?' Stride asked.

'Joe Ralston.'

' "Pecos Joe"? I'm looking for him, yes, but I don't know the guy from Adam. Him and me have never met.'

'I imagined you his friend,' Lambourne said

blandly. 'Ralston owes the Pan Town bank two hundred dollars. He filed a claim on the Powder River, and I lent him the money against the mine's expected profits. It seems his venture was a flop, and he did a moonlight flit. My bank is two hundred dollars out of pocket because of it. I have no wish to take legal action against Ralston, and was hoping that, as his friend, you might wish to reimburse the bank.'

'To hell with that for a yarn!' Stride exploded, incensed past the bearing by what he regarded as the other's cool cheek. ' "Pecos Joe" Ralston is no friend of mine. I've told you once. I'm looking for him, but we've never met. His financial affairs are his own. And yours, in this case. You leave me out of it!'

'Yet there is an agreement,' Lambourne returned, 'and the name Stride appears on it as a guarantor.'

'This gets worse!' Stride complained. 'What kind of legal agreements do you draw up? The name on your paper must be my brother Orville's. Orv has been in the hoosegow since the end part of last year. It's to do with him that I'm seeking Ralston. That brother of mine could have been in no position to guarantee anything when you and "Pecos Joe" drew up your agreement. Ralston had no right to use Orv's name, and you had no right to accept it without prior contact. I'm no lawyer, but I do know right from wrong.'

'Even so, the agreement cannot be discounted,' the banker insisted. 'It is binding on Ralston and, therefore, his guarantor.'

'Bunk!' Stride snorted. 'There's got to be sense in this somewhere, Lambourne. Okay, you've got me here. Are you trying to put one over me?'

'Why on earth would I want to do a thing like that?' the fat man inquired indignantly. 'You doubt my honesty. I see that you do. I'll fetch the bank's agreement with Joseph Ralston. You shall read it, sir.'

'I don't want to read it!' Stride protested. 'I don't want anything to do with it at all!'

'Nevertheless!' Lambourne countered, already on his feet in a state of high dudgeon.

'I've had enough this!' Stride declared. 'If it's so important that "Pecos Joe" pay your bank back, I can tell you where – ' But then Stride cut himself off abruptly, for it occurred to him that he could harm his own chances if he blurted out that Ralston had been seen very recently in the woods near the Powder River. He could do without the bank manager despatching an employee ahead of him and Sandra Aves tomorrow morning and either claiming the Texan's attention first or causing him to light a shuck. 'Botheration!'

'You were saying, Mr Stride?'

'Show me the agreement then!'

'It shall be done,' Lambourne said huffily, an eye upon the table. 'Your whisky – don't waste it.'

The banker turned away. Stride watched the man's wide back receding. Damn the whisky! It looked like good stuff, but the thought of drinking it just now made him feel quite ill. He studied the glass, and a small fly that was buzzing around its top. There was something wrong here. The situation felt strained and implausible. Agreed, the sense of matters had not been lost. There was a certain logic present, and this business concerning the bank's two hundred dollars might be true so far as it went; but he still had this hunch that he had been brought here for a purpose less apparent. Was it possible that Lambourne had abduction in mind? He was mighty keen to have his visitor toss that whisky back. Could the booze be drugged? Stride eased his pistol in leather. The banker would regret it if he was up to some form of jiggery-pokery!

The fly droned softly. Its circuits of the whisky glass grew slower. Then it settled where the rim was damp. Frowning, Stride reached out to brush the insect away, but his fingers were still inches from it, when it suddenly fell away from the lip of the glass and landed on the tabletop beneath, lying utterly still and with its legs in the air.

Startled, Stride placed the tip of his right index finger against the tiny body and stirred it gently, hoping to arouse some evidence of continuing life, but the fly remained totally inert and there could be no doubt that it had died instantly. Suspicious now to the point of certainty, Stride picked up the glass and sniffed its contents, very careful indeed to keep his nostrils clear of the rim, and deep among the whisky fumes he detected a faint chemical odour that reminded him of pear drops.

Great balls of fire! The whisky was poisoned. He had hopelessly underestimated Lambourne's duplicity. Kidnapping had not come into it – murder was the game! The bank manager had tricked him here for a certainty – tricked him here to kill him. Why? It must have something to do with "Pecos Joe". But what? It was completely inexplicable. How could there possibly be an answer to that one? Or had he encountered a homicidal maniac? Maybe the banker specialised in poisoning unwary strangers and burying their bodies in the cellar. He had read of such things. There were a lot of crazy people about.

Taking the stopper out of the decanter, Stride picked up his glass and tipped its contents back into the ornamental bottle. Then, lowering his glass back to the table, he replaced the stopper; and after that he lifted the decanter and shook it until the poisoned whisky was thoroughly mixed with the rest. Then he returned the cut-glass bottle to its former position on the tray, and finally he folded his arms and fixed his eyes upon the door.

Lambourne re-entered the room a few moments later, and a sheet of foolscap depended from the fingers of the banker's right hand. He carried the paper up to the table and, stretching it to the full, got ready to pass it to Stride; but then he noticed that his visitor's glass was empty and, allowing himself a secret smile, said: 'I see you've drunk your whisky. How did you find it?'

'A fine bouquet, sir.'

'Hasn't it?' Lambourne agreed, laying the sheet of foolscap inside. 'Will you have another?'

'No, thank you.'

'I think I'll freshen mine up.'

'Ah, now.'

The banker lifted the stopper from the decanter and, spilling whisky onto that still left in his glass, prepared to drink again, watching Stride intently as he did so. 'I prize this liquor.'

'I know you do,' Stride responded. 'That's why I felt it would be a sin to waste mine, so I tipped it back into the decanter.'

'You did what?' Lambourne asked hoarsely, the colour draining from his face and a knee almost letting him down. 'How dare you!'

'I ought to have let you drink it,' Stride gritted out. 'Perhaps it wouldn't have been murder. I could force some down your gullet now.' He pointed to the dead fly. 'It didn't have to be poison that killed that little critter.' Then he started rising. 'Shall we put it to the test?'

The banker hurled his glass against the wall on the right, then swept the decanter after it, and they burst like grenades, showering the room with diamond facets and filling it with the stink of pooling whisky. 'Get out of my house!' Lambourne shrieked. 'Get out!'

Stride stepped round the table fast. Seizing the black-suited banker by the lapels, he lifted him until they stood eyeball to eyeball. Then he shook Lambourne, quite gently at first, but harder and harder after that, until the man's teeth chattered and his protuberant belly bobbed up and down, propelling him at last into a delicately made Chippendale chair that fell to pieces under the weight of his arrival and left him sprawling amidst its ruined members.

'I know what you attempted here, Lambourne,' Stride said, 'but I don't know why. Whatever you're up to, cut it out!'

Then Stride left the room. He walked down the hall and out into the street, slamming the banker's front door behind him.

FOUR

Stride found his way back to Sadie Aitken's boarding house without any difficulty. Re-entering the hall, he climbed the stairs and passed off the landing into the corridor that served his room. Such was his state of mind that, coming to his door, he drew his sixgun before turning the knob, then gave the door a shove inwards and side-stepped rapidly, half expecting shots to streak out of the darkness beyond; but nothing of the kind happened and, having satisfied himself that no new attempt was to be made on his life, he slid round the jamb and entered his lodgings, holstering his Colt again and fishing out a match. Once more using his thumbnail to strike fire, he went seeking his oil-lamp again, and this time found it easily enough – on a shelf built into the front right-hand corner of his room – and touched off the wick, obtaining a quite respectable light by which he built a new fire from the materials left available on the right of the hearth and soon had warmth creeping back into the cold atmosphere of the room.

Then, sinking into his chair again, he used his

bruised hands to put together a cigarette, which he licked down and placed between his lips, lighting it somewhat absently with a spill. Inhaling deeply, he grimaced at the back of the fireplace, his indignation knowing no bounds. He had let that fat villain of a banker off too lightly. The shaking would serve only to enrage. He ought to have punched Lambourne's head out of shape, then booted him round the room a few times and finally run him by collar and slack to the sheriff's office. But he supposed that he had realized subconsciously at the time – as he perceived consciously now – that he would not have had much of a case to offer against the banker. The whisky containing the poison had been spilled, and the decanter that had contained it had been smashed all over the place. No, he had done about as much as he sensibly could – without risking the rebound of his actions against himself – and could only wait and see what the follow-up, if any, would be; for, far-fetched though it seemed, he was starting to suspect that there was some form of serious crime behind what had been happening to him, and that a link existed between Lambourne and Dan Wall, the gunman. But suspecting – and even feeling a degree of certainty, in so far as all the efforts made against him had obviously been to prevent his making contact with "Pecos Joe" Ralston – he still felt the strongest urge, on conservative grounds, not to get any further mixed up in the doings of evil men than he could avoid. The only duty he really cared about was his duty to brother Orv. Give him a few minutes with 'Pecos Joe', a later meeting in a lawyer's office, and a witnessed statement to take away with him, and all the badmen of the Northwest could go chase a polecat up a crab apple tree for what he cared.

Stride sat an hour or so longer, letting his thoughts go round and round, then went to bed. He took his Colt with him, just in case, and kept it under the pillow. Willing himself to sleep at his lightest, he passed a vaguely uneasy night, but the cold Spring dawn found him reasonably well rested. Getting up, troubled by only the slightest of hangovers, he went about the uncomfortable business of washing and shaving in cold water; and this done – and the clock on the mantelpiece showing a quarter after seven – he pulled on his boots and walked downstairs, the comfortable smell of the house around him further enhanced by the odours of cooking that issued from the kitchen at the back of the building. His mouth watering, he reminded himself that he had paid for lodging only and could expect no breakfast from Sadie Aitken; so he paused for only a moment longer, then gave in to the emptiness of his stomach and went out onto the street, the thought of finding an eating place foremost in his mind.

He located a working man's hash-house at the southern end of town. Entering the place – which was fairly rough and none too clean – he joined the tough and taciturn company of lumberjacks and miners who were breakfasting there. He ordered and put away several fried eggs, three thick rashers of back bacon, and a heap of fried bread and potato slices. After that he drank a pint of coffee and smoked a cigarette; then picked up a copy of the Cheyenne 'Clarion' that was about a week old and began to read.

It was really an exercise in passing time, and most of the news went in through his eyes and got lost at the back of his head; but, on coming to the last page – which seemed to be devoted to territorial gossip and such – he came upon an item that concerned Pan Town and doings along the Powder River. Here Stride tightened up his concentration, and soon saw that Colley Lambourne had a place in this piece of writing. He gathered that the vault of Lambourne's bank was to be used as a storage place for all the gold mined from the Powder River diggings. The precious metal would be allowed to accumulate for certain periods, and then be transported overland to Casper. There it would be transferred to the Union Pacific spur, taken down to Laramie, and then shipped over the main railroad track to the refineries of the East. Naturally, the writer continued, giving way to all the grandiloquence of his calling, the dates of the gold shipments would be 'most closely guarded secrets' and such care would be taken of this welcome addition to the nation's wealth as would 'adequately reflect its worth'. Then the newsman ended with the somewhat redundant comment that, 'while Pan Town could as a whole expect to derive little new business from this arrangement, a spokesman from the Treasury Department had hinted that the guards to be used on the shipments might well be recruited from among the townsmen. Naturally, however, seekers after work in Pan Town should not build too many hopes in this respect, for this part of the development must remain speculative until the government had fully considered its preparations and a definite announcement was made'.

Stride laid the paper aside. All very interesting; but, in his opinion, the people with the power grew crazier every day. Knowing what he did about Colley Lambourne, it seemed folly that anybody should entrust gold to the banker's keeping. Though, on second thoughts, he supposed that Lambourne was really a minor figure in the affair and that the responsibility for storage and security lay with some much higher authority. Whatever the banker's secret involvements, it was unlikely that the information in the 'Clarion's' article bore any direct relationship to what happened to him, Stride, since his arrival in Pan Town. Lambourne could well be all kinds of a swine in some respects, but the most honest of men where his bank was concerned. Folk at every level of the scale were full of such contradictions. Though, having conceded that, he must not be too dismissive – for had he not sensed depths and perspectives behind last night's events that could easily lend truth to his most impossible imaginings?

Leaving his table, Stride casually patted the satisfying fullness behind his waistband and moved outside, certain that the time was still no more than eight-thirty a.m. and half an hour short of the meeting that he had agreed with Sandra Aves. Building another cigarette, he lit up and began treading northwards, determined to see all that was worth seeing as he took a slow walk towards the livery stables. He studied what the clothier and the gunsmith had on offer, took in the selection of goods in the windows of the emporium, glanced at the price of funerals as listed on the undertaker's door, put his nose in at the bakery, gave the butcher a nod, and raised his eyebrows at the display of well-filled underwear that the girls at the whorehouse were putting on at an upstairs window; but his interest was not fully aroused until he reached the Pan Town Bank, where a waggon was pulled across the head of the alley on the northern side of the building and armed soldiers were standing by as civilian labourers unloaded heavy leather sacks and wooden boxes that he imagined to contain large quantities of ore and goldust.

Deliberately slanting his eye across the top of the waggon and down the alley, Stride saw the burdened labourers entering the bank through a side door and then starting their descent of a flight steps that undoubtedly led to the basement. The sight made him reasonably sure that the gold storage of which he had recently been reading had already begun. For a moment he felt a trifle nonplussed by this, since rumour and reality seemed to collide, but then he realized that nothing was at a variance, as the Cheyenne 'Clarion' had provided no dates to place the manifestation of its news in the future.

He kept walking, conscious that the soldiers on guard were watching him, and once more bridled at thoughts of the bank manager and had vague fears for the gold; but just then this idling of the mind ended, for he discovered that he now had the end of the main street plainly in view and could see movement on the ground at the front of the livery barn. He swore under his breath. Sandra Aves was already there, standing at her mount's head and waiting for him.

Throwing the butt of his cigarette into a murky puddle at the centre of the street, he kicked off the catches and picked up to a quick march, covering the last fifty yards of the way with his head held high and his arms swinging. The girl had spotted him, and they exchanged smiles. Void of her paint, she was all the prettier, and there was a freshness about her that belied the unhealthy atmosphere in which she lived and the degrading aspects of her trade. She a good dress sense too, and he admired her brown suede riding habit, yellow silk blouse, tam-o'-shanter, and tooled calf-boots. If ever a harlot had looked worth saving, this one did, and Stride wondered how she had ever become involved in whoring, but that, he recognised, was a presumptuous thought that should never be pursued. Sauce for the goose was sauce for the gander. Each followed his or her own road, and often as not the saint did no more good than the sinner. 'Hi, Sandra,' he greeted, moving up to her and patting her chestnut mare on the nose. 'Are you early, or am I late?'

'I'm early,' she said.

'We'll split the blame,' he responded gallantly.

She smiled. 'Get your horse, Bill. I wouldn't be surprised if we get some more rain later on. There's still a damp feeling in the breeze.'

Nodding, Stride stepped into the gloom of Bright's barn. Whistling up an ostler, he waited for the man to saddle his mount. Then he paid what was owing, and led his horse into the morning light, where he rejoined the girl. Pointing northwards, she mounted up, and he swung into his own saddle; and, watched by one or two members of the livery staff – who unquestionably had a false idea of what their customers were about – they cantered across the Pan Town limits. 'This is the way to the river,' the girl called, when they were a few hundred yards down the trail. 'We'll turn off to the left shortly and ride across country to where the Powder bends east above town.'

'I'm in your hands, lady,' he answered.

They carried on for about another quarter of a mile, then she indicated the turn. Leaving the trail, they passed between two enormous rock-piles and moved out onto boulder-studded grass. The rocks soon became less numerous and gave place to a stretch of open range which had bands of forest and ghostly mountains at its back. Fetching their course further to the left, the girl aimed them towards a spot where the woods appeared less dense and, after casting a cowman's eye across the lie of the land, Stride edged his horse closer to his companion's and said: 'Aren't we just now at the back of town?'

'Yes,' Sandra replied.

He blew through his lips, mildly puzzled. 'Couldn't we have reached this spot in half the time by coming out through the lots?'

'Yes.'

'May I ask why we didn't?'

'I never turn back into town when I start out on a ride,' she explained. 'Jake's Palace is a tall building, and there's always somebody looking out of a window on the top floor. When I ride a horse, I'm a private person, and I don't like being watched – or followed.'

Stride shrugged. He supposed what she had said made a certain amount of sense, though he thought her attitude could be a trifle sensitive. Still, she had the right to her anxieties and habits, so he made no further comment, and they might well have gone on riding all the way to the woods in silence had he not suddenly glimpsed what looked like new waggon tracks cut deep into the rain-soaked prairie before them. 'What'd anybody want a waggon out here for?' he wondered aloud.

'Bill,' Sandra Aves said ironically, 'you're a man of endless curiosity.'

'I'm a suspicious varmint too,' he agreed, halting his mount on the tracks and letting his eyes follow the wheel ruts in the direction of town. 'Reckon those marks end in that little stand of timber just out from the lots.'

'So what?'

'Isn't that grey slate roof yonder the bank?'

'What about it?'

'Nothing, like as not,' Stride returned. 'I'm going to have a look all the same.'

'I haven't got unlimited time,' the girl reminded.

Stride gave her his most charming smile, then he turned his horse towards the nearby trees and, far from sure himself why he was behaving so inconsiderately, thumped his heels against his mount's flanks and went for the timber at full gallop, reaching it in two minutes flat and pulling up in the bay where the wheel-tracks ended. He spotted the waggon almost at once, even though it had been backed under a ledge that jutted from the top of a moss-clad mound of earth and chalk and then covered with boughs freshly cut from the Scotch firs of the enclosing stand.

Swinging down, he strode over to the imperfectly hidden vehicle and pulled some of its camouflage aside, studying what stood beneath with a careful eye, but it was just another low-sided ranch waggon. The buck was empty, and the vehicle was in no sense unusual except for its presence at this spot and that it had been concealed in such a suspicious manner.

'Are you satisfied now?' he heard Sandra's voice ask from behind him and, glancing round, he saw that she must have galloped over in his wake and was now sitting her horse near the tail of his own.

'I will be,' he responded, 'when I find out what lies at the other end of those wheel-marks. Sandra, there's something fishy here.'

'What?'

He couldn't readily answer her. His notions were too vague.

'You see?'

Her air of long-suffering patience was beginning to nettle him. 'You give me a convincing explanation of what *you* see.'

'Certainly, Bill,' she said briskly. 'These plains are

still littered with buffalo skeletons. There are kids in town who go out collecting the bones for grinding up into fertiliser. They get a few dollars for it. This could be their waggon.'

This explanation was so ready, simple, and plausible, that it had the effect of stopping his mind dead. 'I guess that could be it,' he admitted reluctantly; but there was still a touch of the mule about him. 'I aim to look all the same.'

'Come on, then,' she said resignedly.

'Oh, hell!' he grumbled. 'You girls do make such sacrifices!'

'I'm not half a mile from home,' she observed, pulling a face as she looked up into the lowering sky, 'and this is no morning for riding the countryside.'

'You even behave like a girl,' he sniffed, returning to his horse and stepping up.

'That's no compliment,' Sandra complained. 'I am one.'

'I thought you were a woman,' he teased, tongue in cheek.

'You know, Bill,' she said severely, 'you're a lot of fun, but this isn't the time for it.'

'Girl,' he responded half-seriously, gigging off along the tracks left by the waggon wheels and heading just slightly north of west, 'the present time is the only time. For this as well as everything else.'

They moved away from the stand of Scotch firs and out into the plain. Silent now, they covered two miles at a steady trot, and the twin cuttings left by the waggon's iron tyres went on before them, forming perfect sign. Soon the dark mass of the woods ahead broke out in detail, and the still naked boughs of the deciduous trees thrust and twisted amidst the deep green masses of the pinetops.

Before long Stride and the girl came to the edge of the timber. Here the marks left by the waggon wheels turned eastwards. This indicated that the vehicle had almost certainly been brought onto the plain from the trail which they had themselves left something over an hour ago. Stride halted where the sign curved to the right and gazed uncertainly along it until it faded into the grass of the new direction. 'Are we far from where you saw "Pecos Joe", Sandra?' he asked.

'Some way,' she answered.

'Okay,' he said, not wanting to annoy her again and reflecting that, if he wished – or still felt there was a reason for it – he could return to this spot and resume following the tracks later on. 'We'll call that it for now, and get on with what we really came for. If you'll – '

Nodding, the girl set off to the left and, drawing his mount's head round, Stride applied the rowels and began pursuing her, content to stay in her wake as they rode along the boundary of the woods. Their course fluctuating that trifle with such demands as the timber's placement made upon it, they went on like this for the next ten or fifteen minutes. Then, arriving opposite an area where the trees thinned and broken ridges and other formations of stone reared out of the underlying thickets, the girl turned right and rode on for perhaps another two hundred yards, drawing rein where redwoods darkened the ground and a line of previously riven granite became continuous and formed an impassable barrier across the way ahead. 'It was around here that I saw "Pecos Joe",' she said; and then she twisted round in her saddle and pointed through the trees. 'I was back there.'

'He didn't see you?' Stride asked, dismounting.

'I don't think so.'

'Well, this is no place to camp,' Stride commented, glancing around him. 'There's no access to water. Unless there's a stream nearby.'

'Not that I know of,' the girl said. 'The river is on the other side of that stone wall.'

'It's unclimbable,' Stride said without hesitation. 'I think I'll have to look around.' He smiled up at her. 'Thanks, Sandra. You've been a real help to me. Sorry I crossed you back there.'

'You didn't cross me,' she said. 'I was just puzzled by what you were doing.'

'Letting my imagination run away with me, I reckon,' he explained, purposely vague. 'I had some trouble with a man last night, and I guess I can't believe any good of him today. But you don't need to know about any of that.'

'For a man who's only interested in his own affairs,' Sandra Aves remarked, 'you make enemies very readily.'

He considered her words a moment. 'That's how it looks,' he conceded, 'but the hate comes from elsewhere. Once I've got what I need, I'll be gone, and a month from today Pan Town will have forgotten I was ever around.'

'I'll remember you, Bill.'

He grinned doubtfully, giving his head a tiny shake. 'One face among the hundreds. No, Sandra. "Ain't in Nature," as my old pa used to say. You cut off if you want to.'

'I think I'll stick around a few minutes,' she said, 'and see if you do find "Pecos Joe".'

'Suit yourself,' Stride said. 'At that, we might ride back together if I don't have any luck here.'

She made no reply, but sat watching him gravely from her saddle and, not knowing how else to handle it, he turned away from her and began moving in the direction of the barrier rock before him, examining the ground for sign as he went.

Keeping to the right, he soon found evidence which suggested the girl had been correct in saying that she had seen "Pecos Joe" collecting firewood, for there was little sere timber lying about in the area and he also came upon two places where deadfalls had been stripped of all the jutting wood that could be broken off their trunks. He spotted footprints too – not to mention hoofmarks that came and went – and one set of the former appeared to have been impressed since yesterday's rain, for they had gone welt-deep into the carpet of leaf-mould and pine needles which covered the woodland's floor.

Giving way to his curiosity, Stride followed this set of human tracks on its serpentine course through the trees, noting that it never strayed far from the ridge of stone adjacent and betrayed many pauses. Then, after a hundred yards and more of threading dark boles, brush, and berry bushes, he was surprised to see the impressions make a ninety degree turn to the left and approach a cleft in the rock wall that he would have probably ignored but for their presence.

He went closer, and was now downright startled as he perceived that innumerable tracks – some recent and others old – came together at this point and entered the rift, which was several feet across at its mouth and chunked far enough back into the body of the ridge to lose its end in darkness.

Deciding to investigate fully, Stride first cast glances behind and to both sides of him and then stepped into the mouth of the cleft and started his penetration of the shadowy maw behind it. Then, about twelve feet beyond the point from which he had started – though still a pace or two short of the rift's greatest depth – he glimpsed on his left a second fissure that almost equalled the first in size. Turning here, on a floor that was even enough, he passed through the great crack and then found himself in a cave of considerable dimensions, which was dimly lighted by apertures which pierced a wall at the front of the place that soared about twenty feet above the level of the natural door at the rock chamber's rear.

Stride heard movements ahead of him, and came up taut, heart pounding. Horses. He could smell the critters too. And then he heard a male voice say gruffly: 'Keep still you pesky varmints! You want your grub – and I want mine. It's always the cook who's last to feed!'

Fearing that his entry must have been audible, and even that he was visible to the man he could not see, Stride placed his hand upon his gun and waited for it.

FIVE

Nothing happened. The noises went on in the gloom ahead of Stride, but no threat to him of any kind manifested, and he simply stood as before and allowed his body and mind to relax that trifle as he began to seriously question what he had stumbled into.

Quite obviously this was a hideout, and one, judging by the number of individual equine sounds in the vicinity, that was shared at this time by several men, and he could only suppose them to be a gang. For honest men didn't bunch up in this fashion, so he had to assume that he was among desperadoes; and, as he had come here seeking "Pecos Joe" Ralston – who had been seen performing a type of domestic chore hereabouts – he must also assume that Ralston was one of the band.

But, of course, it did not stop there. For, while outlaws had periods of inactivity – and this lot did not *have* to be a threat to the district at present – the fact came up again that "Pecos Joe", an habitual fiddle-foot, had stuck around these parts long enough to suggest that there could be a crime in the offing, and Stride was once more prompted to wonder what it might be; and he could see nothing big enough for a gang to undertake but the theft of the gold that was already being stored in the vault of the Pan Town Bank. This, too, would adequately explain why such strenuous efforts had been made – openly by Dan Wall and only just less so by Banker Lambourne – to cut short his inquiries concerning "Pecos Joe" Ralston, a man who was supposed to have left the neighbourhood in the first place and whose continued presence might possibly betray the gang in the second.

Keeping the tightest hold on his patience, Stride drew the slowest and deepest of breaths, wishing to hell that the man feeding the horses would finish his job quickly and give some indication of what he meant to do next; for though Stride had been enlightened by his latest thinking, he had also been made aware that his life could be in profound jeopardy should he be discovered, since the magnitude of what he suspected that the crooks had in mind would inevitably make them utterly ruthless if they believed their plans to be threatened.

Then, contrary to his previous impressions, Stride realized that the man yonder was in fact already on the move, for climbing noises reached him from the cave's front, and shortly after that he made out a lean male figure ducking through the largest of the high apertures that let some light into the semi-darkness of the rock chamber. Then the man's silhouette vanished from against the sky, and Stride once more had the sensation of being alone.

Now he moved again. Letting air and tension flow away from him, he shifted his left foot to the fore and, groping, set off across the floor of the cave, heading for what he imagined must be the fairly steep slope beneath the apertures that admitted the light. He encountered a small boulder at one point and a patch of rubble at another, but the bottom of the cavern seemed otherwise clear of obstructions; and, keeping the horses on his right – as by the judgment of his hearing – he went on inching forward until the floor made an obvious tilt upwards. Then he adjusted himself for a climb, bending his knees and crouching forward with hands ready to claw a grip, and after that he ascended what proved to be a solid and not difficult slope, soon reaching the hole near the top of the front wall by which the lean man had recently left the cave.

Squaring into the aperture, Stride looked out, his gaze first travelling high – into grey vistas of climbing plains, hanging forests, and befogged mountains – and then lower down to what must be the course of the Powder River, its green-clad banks, and the slope outside the exit that led down into a broad waterside bay that was enclosed by walls of vertical rock and gave the impression of being the kind of fastness which would be approachable only by the river but for the cavern behind him and the external cracks that served it.

Fixing his attention, Stride swept his gaze from left to right across the front of the bay and then back again, taking in every square yard of the ground that was visible towards the water's-edge, but he could detect no movement anywhere below and had to assume that the men present – of whom he had seen only the one so far – most probably had some form of accommodation that was tucked back on the less exposed ground to his right and perhaps sheltered by the eastern semi-arc of the enclosing bluffs. True, there didn't have to be men down there at all – the arrangements did offer other possibilities: like a log-house in the woods or a cave on the ridge – but his whole instinct said that the human part of this hideout was located close to the river and, despite the ever-increasing risk, he made up his mind to go down there and find out who and what was present.

Stride ducked out of the hole before him. The slope outside, like that within, was mostly a ramp of consolidated earth and, squatting, he shuffled down it on his heels, remaining acutely watchful and listening for any sound that might warn of oncoming trouble. He reached the foot of the slope in less than half a minute and, feeling the chill of the briskly flowing river from not more than ten paces away, he jacked himself vertical and faced right, heading now for the cutback which he saw at the acclivity's eastern end.

He started catfooting at the approaches to the indent, and had reason to be glad of his care, for the sound of voices reached him about then and, coming to the place where shelter from the slope ended, he eased his head forward and peeped to the right, spotting a big cave in the face of the nearby cliff and about half a dozen men sitting on a circle of ammunition boxes about a fire that had been bricked round for cooking and over which a gallon coffee pot hung from an iron tripod that was covered in soot.

The men were a rough bunch all right, though mostly trail-honed and fit looking for all their sin-scarred aspects. They ranged from a big, round-limbed redhead with dull blue eyes, through a pair of leathery, tow-headed youngsters who had jibs of the foxy cut and were probably twins, to three longer-boned men of fairly mature years, one of whom was fast greying and wore a cook's apron – the fellow, almost certainly, who had been feeding the horses recently and whose name could well be "Pecos Joe" Ralston now that Stride came to think about it.

'I reckoned he'd be back before now,' the watcher heard one of the foxy-faced pair announce. 'Damn fool, if I do say so! He was in no shape to go huntin' trouble. Never saw a man worse hided. But he'd been simmerin' all night, and I guess it had to be.' The speaker laughed, and not very pleasantly. 'Reckon he's got himself shot, Rory? Maybe that cowboy turned out to have a gun as fast as his fists are hard.'

'Doubt it,' the redheaded man responded. 'Dan'l Wall is one o' *the* top guns. Ain't a handful of men alive who'd stand a real chance against him. What can you tell us about that, Ralston? You know the Stride family, from what we hear.'

'That's stretchin' it some, Rory,' the man in the cook's apron retorted, thus confirming for the eavesdropper that he was "Pecos Joe". 'Ain't never met Bill Stride. His Brother Orville was my saddlepard for a number o' years, but we parted in Denver. There was a waitress there that he took an uncommon shine to. How he come to go to jail – like Dan'l was talkin' about – I ain't got the faintest idea. Like I say, it's no good asking me much at all. And I'm damned if I can say whether Bill Stride is any good with a gun. I never heard Orville tell it so anyhow, and he didn't mind havin' a boast about his family when the mood was on him.'

'Dan'l will be back,' the redheaded Rory said negligently. 'You can't blame him for relaxin' away from this place as much as he can. Wouldn't we be doin' the same, if our mugs weren't known all over? Still, it won't be for much longer. After tonight we'll be well stacked and bound for Easy Street. Down the Powder and into the Platte. Once into Nebraska – '

'Shut up, Rory!' one of the foxy pair yelped. 'Don't you know better than to talk like that? You're givin' out on the whole story!'

'So what?' the redheaded man demanded, sounding aggrieved. 'Who's to hear but us? I imagine it's goin' to be spoke of as smart, us rafting off eastwards while the law's lookin' for us on the land. We got a boss with a good headpiece. I always did figure, Carstairs, that a man worth his salt should turn to crime only once and do a once-for-all job while about it. That's what our boss is on. The first timer just ain't got a criminal record to trip him up. So long as he don't get caught on the job or in the neighbourhood thereof, he stands a mighty good chance of gettin' away with it and living happy ever after. Now ain't that right, Carstairs?

Don't it make sense?'

'I suppose so,' admitted the youngster who had taken the redhead to task. 'But walls do have ears. Me and my brother Saul have proved it. True or false, Saul?'

'True, David,' said brother Saul Carstairs. 'It was loose talk in a hotel bedroom that got our pa hanged down in Las Vegas.'

'This ain't no hotel bedroom, sonny,' Rory soothed.

'The boy ain't so far wrong, McDuff,' affirmed the tougher-looking of the two older men who had not previously spoken in Stride's hearing. 'You do have a loose mouth.'

'I could tighten yours up, Ransome,' McDuff suggested dangerously.

'Cut that out!' snapped the man named Ransome. 'It's mainly because Denny Cocklin and me have obeyed the rule and kept our mouths shut that we still walk free. Him and me have seen some desperate doings in our time.'

'That we have,' the third of the older men, Cocklin, agreed. 'The like won't ever be seen again, Rory. The West's a-changin', boy. The days of our kind are numbered. Give it five years and there'll be a cohort of them Federal marshals ridin' the back trails.' He spat into the fire, his saliva hissing as it turned into steam. 'Every one of them riding marshals is a hand-picked man.'

'Do we have to listen to it again, Denny?' McDuff demanded in a bored voice. 'We know you and Ransome rode with Jesse James and the Youngers. They're all dead or in prison. So it don't mean they was – '

'They got on,' Cocklin interrupted. 'That's what we learned from them. Men in our line of business just have to get on, Rory. Ain't no proper marryin' up on a job if guys start janglin' – like we're janglin' right now.'

'Thanks to you, McDuff,' Saul Carstairs growled. 'Cocklin is only sayin' the same thing as the boss says. We've got to work together as one. We've got to have harmony.'

'Right, laddie,' Ransome agreed. 'Damn right.'

McDuff heaved himself erect, obviously put out. 'Gangin' up on me, hey? What'd I say? You men twist everything and make it come out as something else. Aw, you make me sick!' He gestured disdainfully. 'Well, I can stand my own company, and I think I'll go and get some of it.'

Stride saw McDuff back out from among the men around the fire and start edging to his right. It was clearly the redhead's intention to leave the cave, and Stride realized that if the big fellow headed for the riverside and looked left, he would have the spy in full view. There was nothing for it but to retreat at speed, and Stride did that, keeping low as he backed towards the western end of the slope that formed the next part of his escape route. Then, starting his scramble towards the cavities under the rimrock above which gave access to the cavern in which the horses were kept, Stride slanted a watchful eye to his left, fearing now that McDuff might walk out to the extreme eastern corner of the bay and thus stand at an angle wide enough to take in the entire top section of the incline that the withdrawing man had still to negotiate. But nothing of the kind happened, and Stride completed his climb without spotting further movement anywhere in his vicinity.

Again using the largest of the apertures in the upper cliff, Stride passed into the cave at the heart of the ridge. Standing on the downgrade behind the opening, he paused a few moments to let his eyes accustom to the inner gloom, then began a reasonably cautious descent, moving soon onto the floor below and again keeping well clear of the area in which he believed the badmen's horses to be standing as he made for the light-starred fissure at the left rear of the place, which had been his way into the cavern and must now be his exit from it.

It took him a further minute to circle into the opening; then, back in the open air, he moved out of the rift at the back of the ridge and stood once more among the trees. Gazing to his right, he estimated the position at which he had earlier left his horse and began making for it, a worry that had been largely inactive before now increasing in him, for he remembered what he had heard concerning the expected return to the hideout of Dan Wall; and he feared that he might run into the gunman while passing through the wood or even find the other waiting for him when he regained his mount. Yet it wasn't so much for himself that he was concerned as Sandra Aves. Her danger from a returning Wall could be even greater than his own, and he hoped that the girl had soon tired of waiting for him and begun her ride back to Pan Town long ago. Though even that could have had its hazards if she had encountered Wall somewhere on the nearby grass.

Stride's bump of direction proved good. After walking a hundred or two yards, he saw his mount directly ahead of him through the trees and rejoined it. Sandra Aves was nowhere in sight and, relieved, he took it that she had indeed lost the desire to hang about and made tracks for home. Turning his horse, Stride mounted up and started riding back towards the range. Watchful still, he was ready to slip into hiding at the first sound of movement anywhere close by; but, except for the low and sullen roaring of the breeze in the treetops, there was no noise in the locality, and it seemed to him that the uneasiness which persisted in him must be the result of nerve strain rather than some more tangible cause. He was deliberately working on himself to recover his calm when, on turning between two tall clumps of evergreen, he made out a horse that he recognised as Sandra's standing on a small oblong of open ground ahead and saw the girl's shape lying on the grass behind it an instant later.

Drawing rein, Stride sprang to the earth and walked quickly over to the motionless figure, perceiving now that the girl's blouse was drenched with blood and that her wide open eyes were fixed and dull. One look at that pallid face was enough to tell him that Sandra Aves was dead. Shocked, Stride sank to his knees beside her and, his fingers touching her still warm left hand, studied the source of the bleeding from her breast. She had unquestionably been killed by a knife, and one with a large blade – probably a Bowie – and he was fairly certain that, although the knife had since been removed, it had been thrown at her from a distance rather than stabbed home from close quarters. But whatever the truth of that, the result was the same; for the girl's heart had been cut in two, and she must have died more-or-less instantly.

Stride forced himself slowly erect. He willed his numbed thought processes to free themselves. Wild impulses began to dart this way and that through his brain, but he soon quenched them and started to consider what had happened here. He wasn't too sure of the motive, though common sense told him that the crime had been designed to put him in a bad light, and it also warned that if he packed the body back into town he was going to be required to do some tricky explaining. With that reason foremost, he was tempted to hide the remains for now; but that, in the long term, must suggest guilt and would lose him more than it gained, since a number of people in Pan Town had seen him leave Bright's livery stables with Sandra Aves, and that in itself would be enough to make him chief suspect for her murder if he didn't do his duty by her exactly as society required. If he told the truth about what had happened out here, he should have nothing to fear, and he could unquestionably point the finger at the girl's killer, since he was pretty certain that Dan Wall had murdered Sandra. True, in revealing that much, he would have to tell what he had discovered beside the river, and that could lead to more difficulties; for, while he could swear that crime was imminent – and that he could almost certainly guess at the nature of it – nothing had actually occurred yet by which he could sustain an accusation. And, worse still from his point of view, if he made too much public at this time, he was obviously going to lose all chance of obtaining a statement from 'Pecos Joe' Ralston that would clear brother Orville. What between Sandra's murder and the other criminal activities seemingly emergent, this business was now complicating past any real hope of a beneficial outcome for Orville Stride, and Bill himself was about to become thoroughly entangled in the affairs of others when he wanted none of it. 'Damn you, Orv!' he sighed. But it was too late for regrets.

Pulling himself together, Stride walked up to Sandra's horse and then backed it until it stood beside the body. After that he went to his own mount, untied the slicker from behind his saddle, then carefully wrapped the corpse in it to prevent getting blood all over himself and everything else. Now he lifted Sandra's body and bent it across her saddle; and finally he fetched his lariat and tied the remains securely in place. By this time he felt sufficiently outraged by this wanton destruction of a young life to hope that he would meet Dan Wall on the way back to Pan Town. If they got to shooting, so much the better. But he doubted that he would be granted this kind of relief, for Wall was nobody's fool and undoubtedly playing a deeper game than that. Indeed, Stride had the notion that he was about to do exactly what the gunman wanted him to do – and he was tempted anew to find a less risky course for himself – but there were some situations that were unavoidable, and he seemed to be trapped in one of them right now.

Going to his mount, Stride swung onto the creature's back and nudged it into motion, bending over as he passed the girl's horse and catching up its reins in his left hand. Then, with his own mount advancing steadily and the second following his tow, he rode out of the woods and onto the range again, heading directly for Pan Town across an empty distance.

He arrived back in the place about an hour later, re-entering it through one of the alleys on the town's western side; and he went at once to the sheriff's office, which was situated at the middle of the built up area and on the eastern border of the main street. Stride was conscious of being watched by many pairs of eyes as he halted in front of the law building and dismounted, but he looked neither to left nor right as he tied his horse at the hitching rail and then led the second animal forward and secured it to the left of his own animal and almost opposite the law office door, where a stocky man with rubicund cheeks, a much-flattened nose, greying walrus moustache, steep forehead and cleft chin, had just appeared on the step and was gazing at the yellow-shrouded burden on the horse nearest him with pursed lips and questioning eyes. 'Who is it?' he asked. 'Those legs are a woman's.'

'Sandra Aves from Jake's Palace,' Stride answered.

'By cracky!' the other exclaimed, his gaze dead now and voice passionless. 'How did it happen? Where did it happen?'

'Take it you're the sheriff, sir?' Stride queried.

'George Hurst,' the man on the step agreed, shifting the left half of his leather waistcoat to reveal the sheriff's star on the front of his shirt above the pectoral. 'No need to tell me who you are. There's enough talk about you around the town.'

'Hope it's all good. Bill Stride's the name anyhow.'

'Don't give me any of that,' Hurst breathed disgustedly, puckerings of dislike already apparent on his features. 'Who in tarnation could say a good word for a roughneck like you?'

Stride shrugged.

'I asked you two questions.'

'Know you did,' Stride acknowledged. 'She was knifed. Happened yonder, in the woods.'

'What's the rest?'

'She was with me,' Stride explained. 'We left town together, from Bright's barn, towards nine a.m. I was looking for a guy named "Pecos Joe" Ralston, and Sandra reckoned she'd seen him in the woods, it would've been the day before yesterday. I left her and went off to do some looking – that was when we got to the woods – and was sort of reckoning on her coming back to town; and that was what I thought had happened, when I got back from my hunt round and found her gone. Only I ran across her again shortly after that, lying murdered on the grass near some evergreens. Set me askew, I can tell you. It was a wicked deed, Sheriff, and the guy who did it deserves to hang twice over.'

'Any idea who it was, Stride?'

'I've a pretty fair notion, Sheriff.'

'Who?'

'Dan'l Wall.'

The sheriff stood poker-faced. 'You saw him do it?'

'No.'

'I can understand why folk seem to find you hard to take,' Hurst said sourly.

'I know, I know,' Stride soothed. 'There's a heap more to it.'

Hurst had started nodding absently, but his gaze was slanted towards Stride's horse. 'What's that?' he asked sharply, pointing with a left forefinger that was short and spatulate.

'What's what?' Stride inquired.

'Dripping out of the bottom of your saddlebag,' the sheriff responded, leaving his doorway then and making his way to Stride's mount, where he opened the nearside saddlebag and reached into it, bringing out a large Bowie knife which had a blade of tempered steel that was smothered in blood, some of which had trickled through a weak spot in the bottom of the bag and formed a half-congealed drippage that looked very ugly indeed. Now the sheriff held up his find and asked grimly: 'This your Bowie, Stride?'

'It is not,' Stride said flatly. 'So that was the varmint's game!'

'Maybe you're going to tell me you didn't know it

was in your bag?' Hurst suggested.

'I didn't know.'

'You'd better tell me something better than that,' the lawman snapped.

Stride had no doubt of it, and he did have more convincing things to tell; but he feared that he was not going to be believed now anyway.

SIX

Stride looked on with a kind of questioning interest as Sheriff Hurst carried the Bowie knife slowly to a nearby windowsill and gingerly laid the blade upon it. He was puzzled as to why the lawman should be so exaggeratedly careful over an action that appeared so simple, and was correspondingly startled when the sheriff spun on him and snapped: 'I'll have your gun!'

'Hey, now' Stride protested, his right hand moving involuntarily towards his holster; and the next thing he knew steel cracked against his left temple and dropped him all but unconscious in the mud at the edge of the street.

Unable to move, he lay there and, as from afar, heard the sheriff call: 'You there, Ralph?'

'What's up, George?' inquired an answering male voice from somewhere deep inside the law office.

'Leave that scrubbing for now, Ralph!' Hurst commanded. 'Come out here and give me a hand! I've got a prisoner I want to get into a cell!'

His impressions still of the dimmest, the semi-conscious Stride soon felt the vibrations of the second man's approach. Then he was aware of hands winding themselves into the collar of his coat and a bumping sensation as the sheriff and the newcomer dragged him across the boardwalk in front of the office door, over the threshold, across the wooden floor beyond, and then into a gloomy place at the back of the law building which was floored with flagstones and possessed a faint odour of dampness and unclean bodies. Then, as his rough handling became rougher still, his head and shoulders banged against iron bars and set them rattling, and he had the dizzy impression of being hauled to the further side of a cage, where he was lifted by his shoulders and feet and dumped on a bed of sorts that yielded little to the weight of his arrival. After that, his eyes closed, Stride sensed the withdrawal of the pair who had brought him to this place, and he felt as much as heard the metallic closure of his prison door and the grating revolution of the key that shot a steel tongue into a crude but effective deadlock. And finally he was glad just to let go and allow the pain to work through his skull in ever more definite stages until he was fully conscious again and cognisant of bruised bone and a splitting headache.

For the next thirty minutes he did no more than lie upon his back. He felt too ill to do anything else. But then scrubbing noises from his right aroused a certain amount of new interest in him, and he rolled his head towards the sound and opened his eyes, thus bringing into sight – on the other side of the bars at the front of his cell – a large, athletic man, with a good brow and clean-cut features, who was down on his knees, scrubbing brush in hand, and cleansing the floor of the passage which crossed the end of the jailhouse in which the watching Stride was now being treated to such dubious hospitality. Just then the kneeling man's face came round and, as their eyes met, the captive slowly sat up and swung his feet to the floor. After that he announced with great indignation: 'I intend to have that sheriff's badge for hitting me like that!'

'Don't talk like a fool!' the man in the corridor fired back, rising to his feet and squaring round to the bars, his expression grave and the deputy sheriff's badge shining dully on the front of his loose fitting bottle-green shirt. 'You were going for your gun.'

'I was not!' Stride protested. 'It was sheer trickery on his part. The sheriff wanted an excuse to buffalo me!'

'What if he did?' the deputy asked indifferently. 'It's the best way to get a dangerous man behind bars. From what I've heard, you're among the worst of the wicked.'

'That's what I say!' Stride snorted, paying for his anger with a particularly excruciating pang from the front of his brain. 'A stranger in town gets set on, does a thorough job of defending himself, and is at once branded a villain. That's not fair play, Deputy!'

'When a man knifes a young woman to death he becomes a murderer,' the other reminded sternly. 'The sheriff told me you said yourself that a man who does a thing like that deserves to hang twice over.'

'I didn't kill Sandra Aves,' Stride said. 'Dan Wall did that, and put the knife in my saddlebag.' Then a shocking thought came to him and he added: 'I believe your boss had been told where to look for that Bowie and was just waiting for me to ride in. I'll swear Dan Wall has got his number!'

Obviously on the edge of issuing another sharp rebuke, the deputy sheriff paused abruptly and showed a momentary perturbation – his lips compressing and the air roaring softly from his lungs – but then the rebuttal came, and it was delivered in tones of the grimmest warning. 'Don't you ever say a thing like that again, Stride! You'll only get yourself an even worse name and probably hang a few weeks faster! Whatever you may say, the law in this town is honest law! Its custodians have no truck with rogues and killers! George Hurst is a grade A man, and this is Ralph Parsons, another one, telling you so! Have you got it, you woman-slaying scum?'

'No!' Stride returned adamantly. 'You may be a grade A man, Parsons, but George Hurst isn't. He's the old style lawman from the cowtowns, and no better than the carrion he marshals. A frame's been made for me, mister, and Hurst was just waiting to push my head into it!'

'It's a good job George isn't here to listen to this,' Parsons said. 'By heavens, man, you'd hear a few truths about yourself! Was I you, I think myself lucky he's taken Sandra Aves's body along to the undertaker's.'

'I'm not afraid to say to his face what I've said behind his back!' Stride declared. 'You've got some real crime coming up in this town, Deputy. I reckon it mostly concerns Banker Lambourne and Dan Wall, but who else may be in it is anybody's guess. There's a secret hideout beside the river, and in it a priceless pack of villains are waiting for tonight. I've seen them myself – can give you their names. Those hellions were waiting for Wall to join them while I was playing spy. But he didn't. He came on Sandra in the woods and murdered her instead. Then, figuring my horse was nearby, pulled out the knife he'd used and went and found the critter, shoving the Bowie in my saddlebag. After that, like I suggested, he rode straight back to town and had himself a pow-wow with Sheriff Hurst.'

'You're out of your mind!' Parsons announced; but there was less vehemence about him now, and a smidgeon more than curiosity in his manner – a subtle revelation, perhaps, that hinted he had lately been alerted to rather more than he was prepared to let on. 'You mentioned names.'

'I can give names.'

'Then spit 'em out.'

'Saul and David Carstairs, Rory McDuff, Denny Cocklin and Joe Ransome.'

'The Carstairs twins, eh?' Parsons mused. 'That's interesting.'

'I was expecting you to flare up at the mention of Banker Lambourne's name,' Stride said narrowly.

'A man tires,' Parsons observed. 'Do you expect me to fly off the handle at every impossible thing you say? What that's illegal could a man of Colley Lambourne's calibre be involved in?'

'You're too bright to stand there looking that

dumb!' Stride accused. 'Thunderation, man! You read the papers, don't you? The vault of Lambourne's bank is being used to store the gold taken out of the Power River diggings. I read about it myself this morning.'

'Simmer down,' the deputy sheriff advised, 'and be a bit more respectful. There's no need to get het up with me. It's true what you say. Our bank is being used to store unrefined gold. But that's a government undertaking.'

'Would that worry a gang of crooks?'

'It might,' Parsons said. 'It would mean taking on the Army as well as the law. Have I understood you? Are you suggesting that Lambourne is in cahoots with a bunch of gold thieves?'

'I think there's a very good chance he's their boss,' Stride answered, going on to recount as briefly as he could the basic facts of his visit to Pan Town and his experience at the bank manager's home the night before, and passing at once into an account of what he had actually overheard while eavesdropping at the gang's hideout.

'So they have plans to raft the loot down the rivers and into Nebraska,' Parsons said. 'That's clever. I'm starting to wonder about you, Stride. You're either telling the truth or you're a damned good liar. Could be a bit of both. I'd like something a touch more solid to judge you by.'

'Would a waggon be solid enough?' Stride asked.

'Waggon?'

'If that bad bunch strikes tonight,' Stride pointed

out, 'they'll need transport to take the gold over to the river, won't they?'

'No doubt about that. Gold's heavy stuff.'

'We agree they'll need a waggon,' Stride said. 'Would you like to find that waggon?'

'Where?'

'Close by. Maybe half a mile west of town. There's a stand of Scotch firs. The waggon's hidden beside a mass of chalk and muck at the back of the trees.'

'I know where you mean,' the deputy said. 'That's the best you can do?'

'That's it, I'm afraid.'

'It may confirm your story,' Parsons said judiciously, 'or it may not.'

'You tell Hurst,' Stride responded bitterly, 'and it won't. I'm not arguing that it wouldn't be necessary to see the men I've named using that waggon in a robbery at the bank for my reading of what's in the wind to be fully proved. But, mister, you do ask a lot.'

'Caught as you are,' Parsons reminded, 'innocence takes more proving than guilt. What's worse, I'm only a deputy sheriff. It I start an investigation on my ownsome – '

'Try any but a private one,' Stride interrupted, 'and you won't help either of us.'

'You, a guy arrested for murder, are asking me to go over my boss's head – even to look into his doings.'

'That's right.'

'Just because he clapped the barrel of a gun against your head?'

'Because he knew where to look.'

'It won't do,' the deputy said, giving his head a shake. 'There's blood at the bottom of your saddle-bag. It's there for all to see. That's what told George Hurst where to look for the knife. And even if he did get his information from Dan Wall, it wouldn't prove complicity. It wouldn't prove anything. You must see that. Lawmen take information from where they can.' Parsons made a dismissive gesture. 'No, your story is a separate thing, Stride. If it has truth in it, it could do you more good in the sheriff's hands than mine.'

'Parsons,' Stride said levelly, 'you hesitated a short while ago. If you've some cause to doubt your boss, think on it real hard. For both our sakes.'

'But mostly yours?'

'I guess so,' Stride admitted.

Parsons turned away from the prisoner. He lowered himself to his knees again and, picking up the scrubbing brush, resumed spreading lather across the floor. Then, after working for perhaps a minute, his face thoughtful throughout, he paused and looked up and round. 'I ought to know better,' he said as a kind of endpiece. 'You'd be amazed at what desperate men will tell you.'

Grimacing, Stride turned his eyes to the floor. He could say nothing more. The judgment lay with the deputy, and he didn't appear to believe what he had heard. Not that Stride could blame the other for doubting him. What Parsons had said about desperate men and their stories was true enough; and it would be a disloyal servant who turned on his chief without perfect proof of guilt.

Unhappily, though – looked at from the broader point of view – he had told Parsons everything; and if the deputy repeated it to the sheriff – which seemed highly probable now – the badmen could, by this route or that, receive a warning that their plan to rob the bank vault was suspected and thus be enabled to delay their robbery until some future date when he had been removed by a lynch rope or due process of law. Frankly he feared the former most, for Westerners had the habit of lynching the murderers of young women, but that was merely a detail in a muddle of ebbing hope.

Feeling that every man's hand was against him – and cursing himself for bringing Sandra's corpse back to town as a matter of moral scruple – Stride stretched out on his bed once more. Closing his eyes, he tried to find sleep, but managed no better than a doze, and he was awake in an instant when, around two hours later, there was a low cough at his cell door and he turned his eyes to see Ralph Parsons standing out in the passage.

Looking faintly conspiratorial, the deputy sheriff beckoned to him.

Rising, Stride walked over to the cell door. 'What is it?' he asked in a low voice – for that seemed to be required.

'I'm just going off duty,' Parsons quickly explained, a watchful eye turned to his left and covering the arched entrance to the office that was just the width of three empty cells away. 'The sheriff has the desk until six p.m. Be careful what you say to him. I haven't repeated anything to him that you told me, and I advise you not to either. George Hurst can be a sooner if he gets worried. I'm talking to you like this for your own sake. There's a lot about you I find bothersome, despite all, and I don't want you to get yourself into any more trouble.'

'Big of you, sir,' Stride said ironically.

'I've told you as man to man,' Parsons said shortly. 'The rest is up to you.'

'I guess you mean it,' Stride said. 'Thanks.'

The deputy sheriff nodded curtly, then walked back into the office, and the listening prisoner heard him say: 'He's okay, George. I've made the arrangements for feeding him. Ray Crabbit will bring in his lunch.'

'Thanks, Ralph,' Stride heard the sheriff acknowledge. 'See you in the morning. Andy Bunker has been told off for the night watch.'

''Kay. So long.'

There was no more said, and Stride heard the street door open and shut. Presuming that Parsons had left the office, the prisoner thrust his hands into the pockets of his trousers and faced into the cell. He was puzzled as to why the deputy should have come through and spoken to him as he had. He had to suppose that it had simply been the act of a caring lawman, though he hoped that it might prove more than that. Was it possible that he had influenced Parsons to a greater extent than had seemed to be the case, and that the deputy might still try to do something on his behalf? He couldn't really tell. He had the feeling that much was happening in the background, and that wait and see was the order of the moment.

Stride moved to the window of his cell. This was placed just above the level of his eyes. He discovered that he could look out into the open by standing on the tips of his toes. But the scene outside didn't please him much. He found himself gazing into the jailhouse yard, and at the back of this space the town gallows stood. He studied this instrument of death, shuddering at the thought that, if everything went totally wrong for him, he could be required to make its closer acquaintance. Having got an eyeful, Stride decided that he had no wish to look outside any more, and he was about to return to his bed, when the tread of booted feet announced that somebody was coming through from the office; and he turned to see the chunky, red-faced figure of Sheriff Hurst approaching his cell. The lawman had a tray that was covered with a teacloth in his hands, and he passed it through the slot built into the bars above the lock to permit this service. 'Your lunch,' Hurst said. 'You'd better eat it while its hot. Grub that's half cold gives no joy to any stomach. You should find it all right. They cook a decent meal at Crabbit's restaurant.'

'Thanks,' Stride said, taking the tray.

'How's your head?'

'Still on my shoulders, Sheriff. No thanks to you.'

'You asked for it,' Hurst said, yawning.

'We both know better than that,' Stride returned grimly.

The sheriff twitched a shoulder indifferently. 'I've seen Judge Henry Pouter. We should get the coroner's report later today. There'll be a preliminary hearing of your case tomorrow morning. The court will appoint legal aid.'

'Will that do any good?'

'Ask yourself.'

'I imagine there's hell in the town.'

'Folk are plain stunned right now,' Hurst replied. 'Sandra Aves was no better than she should be, but she was liked. You're up to your neck, Stride.'

'You put me there, Sheriff.'

'You've got your grub,' Hurst reminded, smiling coldly; and then he turned away and strode back in the direction of his office.

Stride carried the tray over to his bed. Seating himself, with the tray resting on his lap, he removed the cloth from the mug and dishes beneath, finding a pork chop and mixed vegetables for his first course and a slice of date pie and custard for the second. Though his appetite was not at its sharpest, he ate most of the food and drank all his coffee, then set the tray aside and stretched out once more, intending to relax and give his digestive juices a chance, but he had hardly disposed himself like this when the sheriff returned and asked for the tray. Rising again, Stride carried the meal things back to the door and passed them through the slot and, as Hurst removed the tray with his right hand, he passed in four well-thumbed dime novels with the other. 'Do you read?' he asked.

'I read,' Stride answered.

'Those books have been through a few hands,' the lawman said. 'I reckon they'll be held by a few more yet.'

Hurst withdrew, and Stride re-crossed his cell, tossing the novels onto his bed. He gazed down on them for several moments, then picked up the top one and opened its cover; and there, on the blank first page and scrawled crudely in pencil, were the words: *Farewell, friend. Marcus Jones, 1st January, 1879. Hope you get a warmer morning for it than this*.

Stride went cold all over. This day seemed to be a succession of shocks. He shut the book and dropped it back on the bed, knowing instinctively that Marcus Jones had made the closer acquaintance of the Pan Town gallows. George Hurst would have made a better torturer than sheriff. Those novels were undoubtedly his library for the condemned. The prisoner was tempted to spit on them. Man's inhumanity to man certainly took some ugly forms.

Stride continued standing there. He matched the throbbing in his head to the beating of his heart. Time dragged by, and the hush in the jailhouse was heavy and depressing. By listening carefully he found that he could pick up the clanking tick of the round-faced clock in the office and blend it with the other rhythms. The tension of these empty hours was enough to kill a man inside. Stride started to sweat. If only something would happen. If only hell would break loose!

Suddenly it did. The semi-paralysed captive heard the street door crash open and what sounded like a legion of damned souls come trampling through it. Devilish voices, female and shrill, screeched his name – coupling it with terrible maledictions and threats – and the hurrying feet moved into the jailhouse, not one whit checked by the outraged bawling of Sheriff Hurst.

Facing round, Stride backed up against his bed. Then he saw them. Numbering about a dozen, they were all female, and ranging in age from their late thirties down to the middle teens – a company of snarling whores, brassy and painted for war. The women were led by Hetty Gage, who held a brand new rope in her hands with its noose slipped and ready. 'There he is, girls!' she yelled. 'Let's have the murderin' hound out of there and find us a beam! If the men of this town haven't got the guts to lynch our Sandra's killer, let's show 'em the women have!'

An egg whizzed through the bars at the front of Stride's cell. It missed his head by an inch and burst against the wall to his rear. A decaying apple followed it, and then a rotten potato, but the latter was checked by one of the bars and flew to pieces, stinking horribly. Now the women shook the cage with their united strength, and it rattled as if it were about to fall to pieces. Bedlam reigned, and George Hurst added his gruff bellowing to the hysterical shrieking of the whores. Stride cringed, hands at his ears.

Then the sheriff's gun flashed at the ceiling near the jailhouse door, and the explosion crashed and reverberated in the confined space. 'What the – !' Hurst croaked, his outrage so total that it knew no words. 'By the – ! I never – ! What is this, Hetty? Have you gone stark staring mad? Get your fat ass out of here, and take those cat-crazy Palace jades with you! I ought to lock the whole bunch of you up, then forget about you till this time next year! D'you hear me? Get out of my jailhouse, I say – get out!'

Hetty Gage and her companions, first sobered by the noise of the shot and now influenced by the sheriff's masterful language, began to glance furtively at each other and look sheepish. Now the younger girls at the rear of the party started responding to the lawman's demands. Their movements accelerating under the threat of his presence, they slid past him and back into the office one at a time, and he cut at several backsides with the barrel of his Colt before announcing: 'I'm going to see Jake Pelman about you hellcats right now! I'll get the lot of you fired, so help me I will!'

'Why, George darling,' Hetty Gage mocked, still holding her position opposite Stride's cell, 'you come right along and do that! Knowing how Jake and you feel about one another, should be good. Buckets o' blood!'

'Hetty!' the sheriff roared.

'George!'

'Don't you sass me, you – ! Get out of here!'

Turning her face to the prisoner, Hetty Gage dropped him the most deliberate and meaningful of winks, then raced for the exit, yelping as Hurst's left hand struck her posterior. Then she vanished from the jailhouse, with the sheriff lumbering at her heels and, after the street door had banged – presumably in Hurst's wake – silence returned to the building.

Whistling quietly to himself, Stride shook his head in wonderment and let the tension tremor away from him. He had foreseen the possibility that an attempt might be made to lynch him but, even though they had been Sandra Aves's sisters in sin, he had never dreamed that it would come from the whores of Jake's Palace. Yet somehow he didn't get it. The women had overdone it a bit. When he came to think about it, their behaviour had been decidedly theatrical. And, regardless of the gunshot and the sheriff's masterful ways, they had calmed down a lot too quickly.

There had been that wink too. In no way had he felt that it came from a woman bent on harming him. In fact he had sensed that the reverse was true. What was it all about?

SEVEN

Stride was still pondering the question, when he heard the clinking of metal on metal and, glancing quickly up at the window of his cell, saw a hand that held a ring of keys waving back and forth just outside the bars.

Enlightened in that moment as to the reason for it all, he went swiftly to the window and lifted his own right hand, passing it into the open air, and the key ring was put into his grasp and the fingers outside fell away from sight. No word was uttered on either side of the wall, and only the faintest sound of retreating footfalls reached Stride's ears. Feeling his gratitude for the risks that had just been taken on his account, Stride faced about and walked over to his cell door.

Stopping as close to the bars as he could get, he listened intently at the office, which remained silent; and then he went through the keys, discovering that there were six of them and that they were numbered accordingly. He reckoned that number one would fit the street door, the next four would lock and unlock the cells, and number six belonged to the back door of the jailhouse, which meant that the key numbered five should open his cage.

He sorted out key number five. Then he passed it through the bars of the door and inserted it into the lock, finding that it fitted perfectly. Using a light but strong grip, he turned the key clockwise, and the lock snapped open and the door yielded in response to his push, the hinges squeaking softly. Though his period of imprisonment had amounted to no more than a few hours, he experienced a wonderful sense of freedom as he stepped out into the jailhouse passage and was tempted to go at once to the back door and let himself out into the yard beyond; but he realized that, once outside, he would be an escaped prisoner and have every man's hand against him. He needed a gun. His own had been taken away at the time of his arrest, and it was vital that he try to retrieve it before doing anything else.

He imagined that his Colt would be lying somewhere in the office, and he moved down the passage and out into the room at the front of the building. He sent glances sweeping on all sides, hoping that the weapon had a resting place in the open, but there was no sign of it around and he could only assume that it had been put into a drawer of the sheriff's desk.

Moving to the desk – which stood opposite the door that opened onto the street – he began pulling open the drawers in the bank on the left of the knee-hole; but, though he rummaged around sufficiently in each, he found no trace of his gun, and it wasn't until he had been through the same performance on the other side of the desk that he found the weapon lying in the bottom drawer. Lifting it out, he tipped its muzzle upwards and saw through the vents at the front of the cylinder that Hurst had removed the bullets from the Colt before putting it away.

Cursing, since an unloaded gun was hardly better than no gun at all, he made up his mind that – regardless of the fact that he could be walked in upon at any second – he must put up with a further delay and make a reload; so, opening the gate at the back of the pistol's cylinder, he prepared to begin prising cartridges out of his gunbelt and start feeding the weapon's chambers; but he had yet to loosen the first bullet, when the worst happened and the street door burst open. The sheriff came stamping in, and the angry expression on his face turned to one of startled amazement as he saw Stride standing before him.

On edge all along, Stride reacted a split second ahead of the other and hurled his revolver at the sheriff's head. Five pounds of steel hit the lawman between the eyes, and Hurst toppled over backwards and lay inert. Springing round the end of the desk on his left, Stride ran to where the sheriff lay; then, kicking the street door shut, he jerked the lawman's pistol and thrust it into his own holster, leaving his own gun where it had fallen. After that he wound both hands into the collar of Hurst's coat and dragged the sheriff across the office floor, heaving him next into the jailhouse, and then along the passage in front of the cages and into the cell which he had himself occupied until a minute or two ago, dumping him at the middle of the floor and finally withdrawing and turning the lock, thus making a prisoner of the man who had been so happy to hold him as one.

Removing the key from cell four's lock, Stride carried the ring to the door at the rear of the jailhouse. He used the key numbered six to let himself out into the back yard; then, leaving the ring behind him, headed for the unfenced ground along the eastern edge of town, keeping the tall shape of the gallows on his left; and beyond that he might have taken himself almost anywhere, but a mount's whinny drew his attention to the back of the gallows and the horse standing there.

Diverting left, Stride made for the animal, recognising it as his own, and he had reached the mount and was preparing to swing up, when he saw a piece of notepaper that was pinned to the padding that jutted from the front underside of the saddle. Checking, he perceived that the briefest of messages had been pencilled on the paper. It read: *Waggon – 10 p.m.* Stride plucked the paper from his saddle and screwed it up. As he pushed it into a pocket, he was aware that only he knew the import of its words, and that, by the same token, only he knew the identity of the one man who could have written them. It was satisfying to know that he had a partner with a brain.

Looking eastwards, Stride mounted up. He reckoned he'd ride that way for a number of miles, then swing south and west, coming north again to re-enter the Pan Town area from the country opposite to that bordered by the restrictive presence of the Powder River, but he had no more than just got his horse moving, when a tiny missile plucked at the thatching on the right side of his skull and he heard the bang of a pistol behind him.

Ducking, he did not question the threat but drove his heels into his mount's sides. The horse stretched into full gallop. Despite his previous plan, Stride found himself forced to go left and northwards. Another shot rang out; and after that two more cracked and boomed. He heard lead whimper past his left ear, and his mount flinched and snorted. For a moment he feared that the brute had taken a serious hit, but the increased power of its stretching almost immediately told a different story. The horse ran now as seldom before, scared as its master was scared, and the rumble of its hooves took on a note of thunder. Nor did it miss a step when the gun banged again in its wake.

It was time to look back, and Stride did so. He saw Dan Wall about two hundred yards to his rear. The gunman stood with his feet apart and his sixgun steadied between hands raised at about the level of his chin. Chaplets of powdersmoke spun around his head and shoulders, and he was still thumbing at his hammer in an effort to find another shot in a cylinder that was empty according to the count. Enraged – doubtless by his failure to score a hit – Wall suddenly shoved his Colt away and shook a fist. After that he faced left and raced into an alley adjacent, making almost certainly for the main street and his horse.

Convinced that the gunman meant to pursue him, Stride drew his mount to the right and gazed once more into the dull and hazy vistas of the east. His horse kept galloping hard, and he let it have its head. There was plenty of country yonder. He could see the slow roll of the prairie breaking into rugged slopes that were dark with pinewoods. A man who knew his business could give a pursuer a rare old run in such terrain. He already had a good lead, and estimated that he could stretch it to the better part of a mile before the chase fully established itself. That distance meant manoeuvring room. Let Wall catch him if he could. He'd run the fellow ragged; and if it hadn't been for the fact that a great deal now depended on his staying alive, he would have taken pleasure in luring the gunman into the heart of the wilds and there staking everything on a duel to the death.

When a mile out from town, Stride glanced over his shoulder again. He saw Wall in full pursuit, though only a little clear of the lots as yet. Once more he turned his eyes to the front. The great fields of grass had opened fully to him now. Wet and heavy, they flowed towards the shadows of tomorrow, and the breeze blew across them off the mountains of the Wind River, full of melt-water chill and the too-green scent of timbertops that had burgeoned without the sun. Everything was low of spirit. If only the skies would rift and set light shafting.

Stride heard the crack of a rifle behind him. He ignored the sound, knowing that it was no more than Wall trying to persuade him that he was being rapidly overtaken; and he asked himself, as a kind of mental exercise, how his pursuer had come to be at a spot from which the fugitive's escape from the back of the jailhouse had been visible. He could only conclude that Wall had been in Jake's Palace while the whores had been talking up their march on the sheriff's office and, becoming suspicious of their motives, had obeyed his imagination after their return and stepped out back to see for himself whether there was anything amiss at the jailhouse. In this manner a mixture of luck and vague anticipation could have been responsible for the spotting, and Stride was content to leave it at that. To try to complicate it further would be seeking for treachery in realms that were too improbable. Life had a habit of colouring events with touches of the bizarre and unexpected.

For now it had to be a straightfoward chase, and the miles added up. Stride felt his horse start flagging. This was inevitable, and he eased down, aware that Wall would do the same if he had any sense. But the gunman was a rash and cruel individual, and he might believe he saw an opportunity where none was present. Stride gave it a minute or two, then cast a glance back. He saw at once that Wall had made the mistake which his nature predicated. Mistaking his quarry's reduction of pace for equine exhaustion, he was now driving his horse with lashing reins and kicking spurs, and there could be no doubt that he was presently gaining ground; but no mount could stand such treatment for very long, and the reckoning must be just ahead; for the land there was sliced up by watercourses which would require some jumping and sureness of hoof, while beyond the eyots and wet meadows were terraced slopes that climbed steeply to the pinewoods which had been visible from several miles back. Still feeding off his considerable lead, Stride calculated that the additional demands about to be made on the pursuing animal would burn it clean out before it reached the highest sections of timber on the benches across their path.

Coming to the first of the streams, Stride uttered a galvanising shout and lifted his horse over it. The brute landed cleanly, gathered itself through a few checked paces, and then rose again, splashing down on less solid ground this time. Now, obeying the bit, it leapt and sprang among the eyots, never putting a hoof wrong and, after two big jumps where the main flow branched at the further side of the marshy ground, came finally to the strip of green pasture that separated the last of the plain from the beginning of the slopes.

Craning, Stride looked for the gunman. He saw Wall about a quarter of a mile away, on the western side of the streams – which meant that the other had now closed the gap by more than half – but his mount's head had gone down, and the animal was obviously labouring. Stride considered it time to take full advantage of his previous craft, and he put his mount to the grade before him and began to ascend, jinking here and angling there – staggering the climb wherever he could – and before long he reached the slopes on which the pinewoods began and turned southwards through the edge of the first trees.

He gazed back and down, the detail of the acclivities below dizzying to meet the silver ribbons that threaded the watermeadows, and he perceived that Wall had progressed little since his last look at him, and that the gunman had in fact halted beside the first watercourse and just started turning his horse about. Wall had given up. Stride had hoped for it – and expected it – but not this soon. He had been certain that the gunman would push his mount to the limit. Why this change of heart? Wall had simply given up *too* easily. There was more to this than met the eye. What could it be?

His horse moving at little better than a walk now, Stride put his thinking cap on. He went over the events of the day, analysing them carefully – and then he believed he had it. He felt pretty sure that Wall had reached Pan Town that morning, over the range that connected the place with the Powder River area, just after Sandra Aves and he had left the northern end of the main street. It was likely that Wall, keyed up for a gunfight, had asked at once after the man he wished to kill and learned that Stride had just gone riding with the Aves girl. It was a fair bet that the big fellow had at once given chase, and seen the girl and the man he sought turn off the river trail and head out into the range. Following still, perhaps curious by this time – or even fearing by this stage that Sandra might somehow know where "Pecos Joe" Ralston was to be found – Wall could have seen them cut the waggon tracks and then divert townwards and discover the hidden vehicle itself.

After that he might well have hung back in distant shadowing and pursued them towards the Powder

River, slowly making up his mind to eliminate – by whatever means might present themselves – what he would by now have perceived as a definite threat to the plan for stealing the gold from the bank vault. Thus, executed in such manner that no third party influence would be readily suspected, Sandra Aves's brutal death had come about, with the charade concerning the Bowie knife as its follow-up. Assuming Stride had got it correct, it had been clever all right – well conceived and opportune – and now Wall was probably gambling that Stride and the unknown helper who had engineered his escape from jail would turn up at the place where the waggon was hidden tonight, expecting to trap, but only to ride into a trap themselves that would promptly be the death of them. Yes, the reasoning fitted in with all the known facts and likewise accounted for the gunman's signal failure to push his pursuit to the maximum. Stride clucked softly to himself. Well, having deduced some inkling of what the future could hold, it was up to him to set Wall's possible switch at nothing and plan anew, hoping to regain the advantage.

Staying high, Stride rode across slopes that became ever steeper and more densely clad with trees. Twisting in his saddle from time to time, he watched the shape of the retreating Wall grow smaller and smaller on the plain north and west of him. Then the riding figure vanished altogether where the land hollowed, and the sighing of the wind emphasized the loneliness of the heights and the emptiness of the country beyond.

Wet, cold, and by no means sure of his own judgment, Stride headed for the southern skyline a while longer; then, responding to his bump of travel rather than the estimates of his conscious mind, he rode down from the high places and entered the valleys beneath, swinging back gradually on the spot that Pan Town occupied in the eye of his mind; but he was still travelling wild terrain when the dusk settled and, had he not cut the trail by which he had originally entered the Powder River district while there was still a small amount of light by which to see, he might have wandered the night away in cuttings where water roared and on low slopes where unclad trees creaked out the agony of their limbs in the airs that came funnelling through the valleys of the west.

So, riding the dark by courtesy of his mount's gifts rather than his own, he came, at mid-evening, to an open view of Pan Town's street flares and houselights and, keeping in mind the possibility that Sheriff Hurst had possemen on the look out for him, left the beaten way while still more than a mile short of the first dwellings and moved to the western edge of the town, following the lots on that side and knowing what he had to do but finding himself in a bit of a quandary as to how best to do it.

His horse plodded slowly northwards through the dark; but that was not to say all was black along his path, for beams of lamplight reached him at intervals from kitchen windows on his right and the less frequent glow of the lantern burning over a privy door also helped indicate his way. At one point he heard a tethered donkey kick up its rear hooves and bray, at another hens cackled softly from their copes, and at a third a dog rushed his horse, giving him a bad moment – only to retreat inexplicably, without uttering a sound.

Then Stride found himself opposite the inner end of an alley which was lighted down its entire length by the fire streaming from a flare on the further side of the main street. Here he halted his horse and dismounted, satisfied that the street light would be a sufficient marker for his needs and, tying his horse to a paling in a nearby fence, he entered the alley and walked to its further end, arriving on the edge of the main street and pausing there in the shadows.

He gazed furtively on either hand. The street was deserted at present, though sounds of music and revelry reached him from Jake's Palace, which stood across the way and no great distance to his right. His eyes steadied on the building. He feared that he would have to go there for the information he needed; he could not call anywhere else. He must find out where Deputy Sheriff Ralph Parsons lived, and Hetty Gage would be the person to tell him. But clearly the problem would be to contact Hetty without getting seen by somebody who knew his identity in the process. It was going to be difficult to achieve that much and, when Hetty's job and prominent place in the public eye were considered, it could even prove impossible.

Just then Stride heard a tuneless whistling from his left. Withdrawing still further into the gloom, he turned his head to discover who was making the noise. He saw the figure of a boy sauntering towards him, and he realized suddenly that the youngster was familiar. Yes, it was his guide of the previous evening, Jimmy Dankworth. Perhaps he could enlist Jimmy's aid in making contact with Hetty Gage. It was possible that the kid had heard of his arrest – and escape – but it was unlikely that the youngster would have any immediate idea of what to do about it. Anyhow, that was a risk that he would have to take and, as the kid moved opposite him – a pile of broadsheets in his hands that he was probably in process of delivering – Stride called softly: 'Jimmy! Got a moment?'

The boy stopped, peering to his right. 'Who is that?'

'The man you called on yesterday evening.'

'Oh, it's you, Mr Stride,' Jimmy identified, his voice guileless and free of all suggestion that he had heard anything of the day's events that had involved the man in the shadows so disastrously. 'What can I do for you, Mr Stride?'

Then Stride, who had been straining his mind throughout the day in one effort after another to be clever, saw the obvious and realized that he didn't have to bring Hetty Gage into it at all. The risk of asking the boy what he needed to know in a direct manner could be no greater than if he approached it indirectly through the saloon woman. 'Can you tell me where Deputy Sheriff Parsons lives?' he asked.

'Why, sure,' Jimmy replied. 'On your right. Four doors along. I'm going that way; I'll show you.'

'Good fellow,' Stride said, moving into the street

and picking up his step from the boy. 'I didn't dream you'd ever by my guide again. Delivering the news, are you?'

'For Claudius Holroyd, yeah,' the kid agreed. 'He's got a new press.'

'You don't say.'

There were moments of silence after that, and their feet sloshed muddily between the light from one flare and the next. Now Jimmy Dankworth stopped and pointed to a gate on his right. 'That's where the deputy lives.'

'I'm obliged, Jimmy,' Stride said, fishing a quarter from his pocket. 'Here – buy yourself some candy.'

'Thanks, Mr Stride,' the boy responded, taking the money and shoving it away. Then he brought his voice down to a conspiratorial level and added: 'Hope you know what you're doing. That deputy is a hard man.'

'Reckon I do, boy,' Stride chuckled wryly. 'If it should turn out I don't, I'll remember what you said.'

'You must know, sir,' Jimmy said, sounding as if he had had his fifty-first birthday last week. 'Goodnight.'

'Goodnight, Jimmy,' Stride answered, conscious that the kid knew all that mattered and that he had never been in safer hands.

Stride turned to the gate adjacent. Opening it, he walked down a short path that was lined with bushes and came to a porch. Entering here, he knocked on the door beyond. Within moments, the noise of approaching footfalls echoed, and the door swung inwards and Ralph Parsons' big shape loomed on the threshold. 'Sorry about this, Parsons – ' Stride began.

'Is that you?' the deputy interrupted aghast. 'What the blazes are you doing here, man?'

'Could tell you better indoors.'

'Come on in, Stride!' Parsons snapped. 'Look sharp!'

The deputy stepped aside. Stride passed into the hall, and the lawman shut the door behind him. Then Parsons led his visitor across the body of the house and into the clean but somewhat sparsely furnished kitchen at its back. Going to the scrub-topped table, the man turned up the light – which was burning low – then walked to the hearth and, turning his backside to the fire, placed his hands upon his hips and prompted: 'Now?'

Stride nodded. This had to be done without preamble, and he explained to the deputy how Dan Wall had appeared on the scene at the time of his escape from the jailhouse, told of the chase that had followed, how relatively easily the gunman had given up the pursuit, and what he, Stride, had deduced from that action. 'There's no chance of this being a straightforward matter any more,' he concluded. 'We're not going to stick up the members of a gang and simply make arrests. With Dan'l Wall unsure of how much we know – and therefore trying to cover every move we may make next – we must have a fight on our hands. We need help, Parsons. Can you call on a few trustworthy guys who are prepared to bring their guns and take a risk?'

'I don't know,' Parsons replied, doubt radiating from his entire person. 'I keep asking myself how I could've done what I've done, and what I've let myself in for. Really, I don't feel much different now from when I scoffed at you this morning. But I went and looked for that waggon you spoke of, and found it; and I had to give weight to the names you'd mentioned – like the Carstairs twins. Them and Rory McDuff have been reported in the district. As a matter-of-fact, I'd also glimpsed George Hurst in very private talk with Dan Wall not three-quarters of an hour before the sheriff arrested you.

'Now that was a sizable body of reliable information, Stride, and I guess I decided to take a chance on you and that big gold theft that you think may happen. I met Hetty Gage in the town, and she just couldn't believe you'd harmed Sandra Aves. Hetty and Sandra were pals, and it seems Sandra told Hetty, very much on the quiet, that she liked the look of you and thought you might be partial to her. Anyhow I told Hetty that you swore you'd been framed and, after some more talk – which we won't go into – suggested how her and the girls from the Palace might stage a riot and steal the sheriff's keys from his desk-top in the process.' He paused, as if uncertain of his point and how to go on. 'All that I did on my own responsibility, Stride, and I'm not looking for thanks, but there could be error on my side – since the evidence that George Hurst is actually backing crooks stays mighty thin – and, not to labour it, I'd be the worst bastard unhung if I asked help from men in this town who've got wives and kids and it later proved that I had skirted the authority of a sheriff who was guilty of no real crime. I've aided a man of some ideas but no exemplary character, and I could end up sharing the same cell with him. Only God knows the end we serve half the time. Do you savvy, Mr Stride?'

'I savvy, Mr Parsons, and I don't disagree with you. I'd much rather do my own dirty work, but it's only being sensible to wonder if two men have a chance against seven or more. Besides, a big robbery concerns the whole community, and we owe it to other folk to give them the opportunity to help us.'

'You make a good argument there,' the deputy sheriff admitted. 'But I'm not sure that it's a fair one.'

'Fair!' Stride echoed. 'When was this ever a fair world? We have us a situation, sir. We either meet it the best way we can – or we simply meet it.'

'I figure we'll just have to meet it,' Parsons said shortly. 'If, as you suppose, Wall is expecting us to do one thing – but we go out and do another – that must place the greater power with us for now.'

'Trouble is,' Stride sighed, 'I've found Wall as quick on the uptake as we – ' He broke off as he glimpsed a briefly reflected movement down the left-hand edge of the undraped glass of the window opposite him; and, galvanising, he dived straight at Parsons and knocked the deputy sheriff to the floor as a pistol roared outside in the night and glass burst into the room and flew.

EIGHT

Stride rolled on the hearth. Retaliatory thoughts struck through his mind like lightning. He was barely aware of drawing his revolver and triggering his first shot in reply to that which had just shattered the window. The gun outside promptly blazed a second time, then kept lancing fire, but there was a wild quality about the detonations and lead spattered the hearth and fireplace, smashing a bar of the cast-iron grate and also splintering the mantelpiece with ricochets and bringing down plaster elsewhere.

The pistol in the night fell silent after a final roar. Stride saw a shadow move away from where the last gunflash had originated. He blasted at the centre of the spectral image, but the shape was travelling faster than his eye could adequately follow and he knew at once that he had missed. Scrambling off the floor, he lunged towards the still intact glass at the middle of the window, standing with the lamplight at his back as he peered out into the night and hoping that the would-be killer might still be close enough to afford him another shot; but his action proved a folly, and almost cost him his life, for a second gun ribboned out of the darkness and lead kicked at the slack of his coat, missing his flesh by a hairsbreadth.

Recklessly perhaps, Stride stood his ground, fanning now at the spot from which the last gun-flame had struck at him. He heard a thin scream rise through the grinding roar of his Colt, and then the thud of a heavy body falling. Stepping aside now, Stride ceased firing, and the sudden hush brought in the sound of rapidly withdrawing footfalls from the edge of hearing. That, the listener imagined, would be the man who had emptied his pistol into the kitchen getting away. It was already too late to give chase through the night, and Stride dismissed all idea of it. He looked instead at the floor on the left of the hearth, where Ralph Parsons was looking up at him, legs spread, upper body braced from the rear on his palms, and an expression on his face that still showed startlement. 'You okay, Deputy?'

'I guess so,' Parsons answered, suddenly shoving himself erect and casting an aggrieved eye into the damaged quarter of the room. 'Who did – ?'

'Wall!' Stride interrupted impatiently. 'I was trying to tell you how quick on the uptake he is. He was a jump ahead of me again. But there were two of them out there. I dropped one. Bring the lamp. Let's go out and see who?'

The back door was situated towards the rear right-hand corner of the room. Moving to it, Stride raised the latch and stepped out into the kitchen yard. Parsons followed him within moments, the oil-lamp from the table lifted, and a ring of light fell about the figure lying on the ground a short distance beyond the rear wall of the house. Cocking his revolver, Stride watched for the smallest sign of life over there, but none showed itself, and he began a slow advance on his supine victim, recognising Rory McDuff and perceiving that the redhead had been hit just above the bridge of the nose and brained by the rising slug. The outlaw was dead for a certainty, and Stride eased his hammer to half-cock and started reloading the fired chambers of his weapon, gesturing for his companion to move up closer to the dead man.

'Nice going,' Parsons said, real approval in his voice. 'That's Rory McDuff, son-of-a-bitch first class!'

'I know it is,' Stride replied. 'So far as I'm concerned, he's just an enemy we shan't have to worry about again. But the other guy was the important one. I figure Dan Wall must have worked out that you were the only man who could have helped me today, and then judged that, on account of how the afternoon had worked out, I'd visit your house this evening and propose a change in our plans. I expect he was hoping to nail us both before we could even start to become a real threat.'

'He'd have managed it too,' Parsons reflected, 'if you hadn't had your wits about you. Everybody knows Wall has a sound head on his shoulders.'

'He doesn't miss a trick,' Stride growled. 'I've got it pegged those crooks are at the bank now. McDuff being here suggests the rest of the bunch rode in with him.'

'Could be,' Parsons allowed. 'But they're taking a chance if they're doing the job this early.'

'Don't lose sight of the most important fact,' Stride reminded. 'You don't have to make any noise to open a bank when your boss has got the key.'

'That is a fact,' the deputy sheriff acknowledged. 'Though it still takes a heap of swallowing about Colley Lambourne.'

'Not to me it doesn't,' Stride rasped. 'Where do you keep your horse?'

'At the end of my patch,' Parsons answered. 'I've got my own stable there.'

'You'd better saddle up,' Stride advised. 'My mount is hitched to a fence a short way up the lots. It could be we'll need our horses.'

'Could turn out we're wasting time on spec,' Parsons observed.

'There's a chance of it,' Stride conceded. 'But loading up that gold will take time and effort. Those crooks won't have their waggon standing that close to the rear of the bank. The lots get in the way.'

'Reckon they allowed for that bungled drygulching?' the deputy asked. 'The sound of shots was always going to bring folk out – if cautiously.'

'You've got a sound point there,' Stride mused. 'The more need for your horse.' He fully lowered the hammer of his gun, shut the loading gate, and holstered the weapon. 'Has George Hurst got a posse out hunting me?'

'No,' Parsons said. 'The sheriff's at home, nursing his skull.'

'Maybe he plans to take out after me in the morning.'

'Maybe. But – it is remiss.'

'Could be significant,' Stride reflected. 'I'm going on ahead. We'll soon find out if he is involved.'

'I'll light you down to the stable,' Parsons said, and proceeded to do just that, holding the lamp before him as they left McDuff's corpse and he led the way to the bottom of the garden, where his timber-built stable stood revealed.

Here they parted, the deputy carrying his lamp into the stable and Stride turning right and hastening up the lots, his run soon carrying him past the spot where his horse was tethered and on into the ground behind the bank. Since there was a strong probability that the badmen were operating nearby and most likely had somebody on watch for him in the immediate vicinity, he was forced to slow down at this juncture and go ahead more circumspectly, but he soon got the feeling that he was in no danger and quickened his pace again as he approached the alley which linked the lots with the main street at the bank's northern end.

Pausing, he gazed along the alley, seeing that it picked up only a small amount of light from the nearest of flares on the main street and lay between walls like a ribbon of black crepe. Detecting no movement down its length, he entered and padded along it towards the side door through which he had seen the gold being carried down to the bank vault that morning. The door was shut, and near it all was still. Stride moved on until he reached the main street. Here he checked partially; then, as the kind of precaution that would exhaust all possibilities, turned right and crossed the front of the bank, squaring round the building's further end and following the alley there back to the lots, again without coming on any trace of the thieves. He turned left now, and in that moment was aware of a lucky circumstance, for the sky had just broken and moonlight begun streaming dimly into the spreading rift at the centre of the heavens. Purposing to rejoin his horse, he hurried back in the direction from which he had lately come, no sooner reaching his animal than he was joined by Ralph Parsons, who was leading his own mount from the bit. 'What cheer?' the deputy asked.

'The bank is dark and silent,' Stride returned. 'I can find no trace of the gang anywhere.'

'That means they've almost certainly carried out the robbery,' Parsons said.

'That's how it looks,' Stride agreed. 'It seems clear now. Trying to kill us was last on the list. They wanted to erase all risk of pursuit. Rafting a cargo down the river may be smart – but it's also slow.'

'Let's try and find them,' the deputy urged. 'They can't be far away.'

They mounted up. Stride took the lead and headed westwards off the lots. Within minutes they were well out on the range and riding towards the Powder River over much the same line of travel which Sandra Aves and he had pursued that morning while following the waggon tracks in the direction of the riverside woods.

The drenched soil echoed dully to their passage,

and the night remained a pit of gloom in the open spaces. Visibility, despite the presence of the moonlight, was no more than a few yards. Again Stride felt a vague anxiety. While he was pretty sure that the deputy sheriff and he were taking the correct action, he couldn't shake off the notion that this chase was somehow going to disappoint and, after four miles of what seemed like abortive riding, he finally allowed some instinct to drive him to a primitive measure in which he had little faith; and, calling on Parsons to rein in, he did likewise and sprang out of his saddle, crouching in the wet grass as his soles came to rest and putting an ear to the ground.

Straining his senses, Stride at first picked up only the sound of the wind passing over the land; but then, from away to his left and clearly at no great distance, his eardrum detected the kind of faint rumbling noises which could only be transmitted by the turning wheels of a heavy vehicle. Rising, satisfied that he had located the crooks, Stride climbed back into his saddle and said: 'The waggon's to the left of us, and not far away.' Then he drew and cocked his revolver and, hoping to provoke a reply that would pinpoint the thieves, triggered in the general direction from which the wheel sounds had come.

The response was almost immediate and gratifying. Tiny flashes of scarlet fire darted at Stride and his companion from the darkness of the southwest and perhaps a hundred yards away. The explosions had a rending quality, and the echoes lashed out at unseen hills and came rolling back as vibrations smothering and metallic. Hacking at his mount's flanks, Stride spoke a word to Parsons and then rode straight for the flashing gun muzzles, his own revolver readied and pointing skywards near his right ear. The outlaw weapons went on spitting, and he heard the odd bullet sing past him, but he ignored the shooting – knowing it to be as blind and haphazard as his own shot had been – and just kept closing in, and it wasn't long before he heard the grinding of axles and the snorting of horses.

Through the heavier sounds came the hissing and cracking of a whip, and a voice that was becoming frantic bawled and swore at the horses pulling the waggon, which remained more or less invisible in the ground shadows. In so far as he could be certain of it in his small acquaintance with the driver's tones, Stride believed it was "Pecos Joe" in charge of the vehicle, and he hoped to goodness that the man would survive the action to come – perhaps with the kind of wound that would immobilise him and make him ready to co-operate – but in a parblind situation like this, the participants could only accept their targets as they came. If disaster did overtake Ralston, brother Orv would just have to grit his teeth and be understanding. Anyhow, the leopard didn't change its spots and, perhaps fearing that truth, Orville Stride might have recognised the risk that his bosom pal would be involved in some skulduggery when he had asked his brother to go forth and plead his case.

The waggon loomed, but only as a manoeuvring shape that came and went in the murk. Estimating its position, Stride rode at it, but then a rider cut across his path and forced him to rein back with all his strength. His mount almost toppling, Stride reeled to his left, yelling his fright as a gun was thrust at him from the right and touched his coat before going off. He felt the bullet sting the flesh over his hipbone on that side, but he was again lucky and it did no damage worth the mentioning. Reflexively, he blasted a reply, his shot angled acutely to the rear, and a sobbing cry told him that he had given far worse than he had received.

'Saul!' a voice called anxiously from Stride's left. 'Are you all right?'

'Hell, no!' came a response choked with agony. 'I'm done for, Dave! My backbone has been shot – !' Next moment the night filled with the sound of a horse tipping onto its nose and the thud of a man's body coming to rest on the ground beyond it.

'Saul! Saul!' Dave Carstairs' voice was panicking now. 'Saul, for God's sake answer – !'

'Shut up, kid, damn your eyes!' an older voice snarled, unquestionably from the retreating waggon, and then the boom of a rifle told of a second man riding the vehicle in the driver's company.

Getting his horse in full motion again, Stride made for the point from which the long gun had blasted. At the same time he was aware of an exchange of shots on his left, fire streaking back and forth between two horsemen – who could only be Dave Carstairs and Ralph Parsons – and a coughing gasp followed the last of the explosions, and Stride heard the sound of another body hitting the ground. 'Parsons?' he asked tightly.

'I'm whole,' the deputy answered. 'Any more riders your way?'

'I don't think so,' Stride called back.

'Then that just leaves the waggon,' Parsons commented, galloping parallel with him.

'Seems so,' Stride agreed. 'There's something wrong here.'

'In what way?'

'There ought to be more of them.'

'The others could have gone on ahead,' the deputy suggested. 'Where's the raft?'

'I don't exactly know,' Stride admitted, shocked to hear himself say it; for he hadn't given too much thought to that all important detail previously.

'That's a nice yarn!'

'It must be near the riverside hideout!'

The silence from the deputy sheriff's direction was like an accusation.

The man was right too. The raft didn't *have* to be where Stride supposed. But that was something that would have to work itself out. Stride couldn't worry about it right now. The task for the moment was to bring the waggon to a halt, and he lashed his mount with that alone in mind.

Overhead the moonlight brightened, and the waggon came into full view about forty yards in front of the chasing men. The rifle on its driving board bellowed and roared; but, though he detected more than one near miss, Stride did not reply. He kept goading his horse closer and closer to the rifleman, determined to do the job with one bullet when he got near enough – always assuming that Parsons didn't do the necessary first.

They were nearing the limit of the grassland by this time, and rocks, lying both single and heaped, were beginning to reveal themselves ahead. Stride could see the danger, and he hoped that it would force the driver of the waggon to slow down, but the man kept his whip cracking and went on as fast as ever. Then the almost inevitable happened, and the crash of a wheel hitting an obstruction was heard. Stride saw the waggon bound several feet into the air, weaving back and forth, then thud down a short way beyond the rock which it had just encountered. Now it swerved to the right, tearing free from the team, and met another boulder – one so shaped that both its off-side wheels rode up the flat but steeply canted top – and this time it turned completely over before slamming down square again with such violence that it flew half to pieces prior to digging in its tongue and ploughing to a halt. Of the two men previously aboard the waggon, Stride could see nothing now, and he feared that both must have been sent rocketing and come to rest with killing force. Now he brought his horse to a stop and, springing down, ran forward to find out whether this were indeed the case.

He came upon the driver. The man was lying on his face at about the spot where the upheaval of the accident might have been expected to dump him. Stride felt for the wrist and neck pulses, but these were still; and, as he tipped the body over, the limp rolling of the head told its own story. The driver had indeed been "Pecos Joe" Ralston. His neck was broken and he was dead. The disaster which Stride had been afraid might overtake the man had occurred, and brother Orv would have to accept that no proof of his innocence would be coming from that source.

Looking round, Stride perceived that Ralph Parsons had also dismounted. The deputy sheriff had walked onto the ground at the further side of the wrecked waggon's final tracks and clearly located the second man from the vehicle's driving board, for he was crouching over a black shape on the ground before him and appeared to be making an examination. 'How is he?' Stride inquired.

'Dead as a doornail,' Parsons replied, craning over his right shoulder. 'How about yours?'

'Same,' Stride answered, walking over to the other and looking down as the deputy sheriff struck a match above the face of the corpse before him. 'Joe Ransome. Once seen, never forgotten.'

'You're a cowboy, aren't you, Stride?'

'That's the job I do. Why?'

'If you get paid out on the rewards for these hombres,' the lawman explained, 'you should have about enough to set up in the ranching business for yourself.'

'With my luck!' Stride scoffed. 'Come on, Deputy. We have to find that gold.'

'So we do,' Parsons agreed, jerking a thumb to his left. 'It was back there the waggon did its revolution.'

'A cowboy would never think of a word like that,'

Stride said admiringly, facing round then and walking onto the ground indicated, where he began a quartering that produced a disquieting lack of results.

Parsons went to it as Stride's kicking around slowed up, but his search was no more successful than the other man's had been. 'I suppose it could've happened further back than I thought,' he commented.

'No,' Stride said. 'I've had the feeling all along there was something here that wasn't quite right. Wall has out-smarted us again. We've been fooled.'

'Are you saying the waggon was empty all along, Stride, and its presence on the range just a diversion?'

'That's what I'm saying.'

'Then where is the gold?' Parsons demanded.

'As to that,' Stride said glumly, 'I was thinking of asking you the same thing. Your guess could prove better than mine.'

NINE

Stride and the deputy sheriff recovered their horses; then, by tacit agreement, they mounted up and let their animals drift towards each other, heads down in the fitful moonlight. Drawing rein as they came opposite, they sat for a few moments in silence, the nose of Stride's horse near the tail of his companion's.

Parsons said: 'The gold could still be in the vault at the bank – if the idea was simply to draw us out of the way.'

'Can't see it,' Stride responded. 'That shooting in town had to put the cat among the pigeons.'

'Has it been taken overland?'

'This trick strikes me as a hasty precaution against the possibility of a foul up,' Stride remarked, slowly shaking his head. 'No, when I first heard about the raft, the guys doing the talking hadn't the faintest idea I was listening and obviously regarded it as the key to their plan. It's not something they'll readily change. I imagine Dan'l Wall had it figured that the four men with the waggon ought to have been enough to put paid to you and me.'

'Very good,' Parsons said. 'We'll accept that the raft part of it holds. So if the gold has gone to the river, we have to decide at what point and how carried.'

'Pack animals,' Stride said. 'They could have used their own mounts. It's likely they had those belonging to Ransome and Ralston too. Possibly George Hurst's also. Five or six horses. Over a short distance, that many nags would make no bones about carrying a quarter of a ton of gold ore.' Bending forward, he gave his mount's neck a thoughtful pat. 'How far is it from Pan Town to the Powder River?'

'Two – two and a half miles.'

'Does that waggon have anything to tell us?' Stride wondered. 'It must have had an owner before those crooks came by it. I reckon they bought the thing from somebody. It wouldn't have been worth endangering their plans by stealing a thing like that. I wonder what reason they gave the seller for wanting the vehicle? How about for carrying logs? Obviously they wouldn't have told the full story of their intentions, but I'm talking about the logs they would have had to cut for building their raft.'

Parsons snapped his fingers. 'Abe Buckle's farm,' he said. 'The place is on the river, just to the right of the Midwest ford. That's the likely source of the waggon. Abe is a sharp dealer, so he wouldn't ask many questions. You need the right kind of timber for raft-making too. Good round trunks, but not too hefty. There's a large stand of red firs along the riverside – about a mile east of Buckle's farm. Does that tell us something more?'

'Nicely,' Stride said. 'Sounds pretty near the mark. So how far's that from here?'

'Eight miles, give or take,' the deputy answered, looking up at the sky, where the moonlight was misting into an increasingly narrow wedge of clear sky from the fringes of an enormous raincloud that was pushing in from the southwest. 'I wish it was daylight.'

'There's a whole long night between us and that,' Stride said.

'I suppose we ought to pick up the dead and pack them back to town,' Parsons said.

'You're the boss here, Deputy,' Stride remarked, 'but I reckon that would be a lunatic thing to do. We've got our teeth in, so why stop biting?'

'We're still an army of two,' Parsons reminded. 'I'd feel a lot happier about asking for help now, and pretty sure of getting all we could use.'

'This army of two has already proved an effective one,' Stride reminded. 'It's five for us and none against – if you discount Sandra Aves.'

'It's a fair score,' Parsons acknowledged, 'however you look at it. 'But pride and impatience go together.'

'Likewise delay and failure.'

'Going back to town could lose us a couple of hours.'

'Half the night,' Stride said bluntly, 'and well you know it.'

'Possibly,' Parsons admitted, 'between all the talk there'd be and getting men out of bed. I'm still as little sure that I'm wrong as you're right. But let's get on with it, and hope that the luck stays with us for as long as we need it. If we follow the edge of the woods eastwards, we must get to where we want to go.'

Nodding, Stride turned his horse tightly to the right; then, kicking with his heels, brought the brute even with Parsons' mount – which was already trotting ahead – and they veered left and moved through the rocks scattered about the area, fetching right and heading eastwards as the woods revealed their black presence where the moonlight reflected off the tree-tops along the boundary of the range.

It was a matter now of exercising patience and enduring the ride. Presently the skies closed over again, and once more it was night indeed, with a new wind keening and moisture blowing through it. There was no question of galloping the horses in these conditions; a safe trot represented the fastest progress; and the dreary miles fell back but slowly, with nothing to encourage the mind until hooves clattered briefly on bared rock and the deputy remarked that they had just crossed the town trail above Midwest ford.

Still guided by the presence of the trees, the two men passed into what Stride had gathered would be the second and much shorter stage of their ride eastwards, and only minutes later broken soil on their right and the glow of a barn lantern on their left indicated the position of Buckle's farm. After that they went on for a while longer, and then, with an angry, half-defeated abruptness, Parsons said: 'Hold it, Stride. We're at where we were aiming for. But what the hell good we're about to do, I don't know. Have you got a cat's eyes?'

'I reckon mine are about the same as yours,' Stride said irritably, listening to the low roaring of tall trees as the wind gusted among their highest boughs. 'The best thing we can do is dismount and head for the river. When we reach the water, we can turn which direction you like along its brink and walk – hoping for whatever suits us best.'

'It was never going to be better than that,' Parsons conceded.

'Two men or three dozen,' Stride said emphatically, alighting as he heard his companion dismount.

Stride faced left. Gripping his horse near the mouth, he gave the lead, and felt the wind cease its buffeting and the wetness of the rain pass from the air as the pine trees of the present stand built a kind of wall around them and put a roof of sorts above their heads. It would have been easy to lose all sense of direction while groping through the darkness connecting the boles – and Stride found it hard to place any trust in the little that he believed he did have – but he kept as nearly to a straight line as he could, not hesitating to trample through the middle of light undergrowth and only pausing to feel his way around obstructions when they proved of a major kind. If his confidence faltered, his nerve never did, but he was relieved all the same when he heard the swift washing of rain-swollen waters ahead and knew that he had found the river.

Cocking an ear, he listened into his wake for Parsons, realizing now that he had been so intent on finding a path through the benighted wood that he had not given a thought to keeping in close contact with his companion, but he now picked up sounds from the deputy and the other horse and estimated that they were no more than a few yards behind him. 'We're approaching the river, Parsons,' he announced, keeping his voice low but clear. 'Can you hear it?'

'I can hear it,' the deputy replied.

'What's it to be – left or right?'

'Left,' Parsons responded. 'Abe Buckle's property is on that hand. If we reach his yard without coming across any sign of the crooks, we can then retrace our steps and head down the river.'

'That's the best way,' Stride approved, slanting to his left until he made out the undoubted presence of the water just a pace or two before him. Here he squared round fully and began to follow the riverbank westwards.

There were now no obstacles to progress, for the trees were few and the undergrowth almost non-existent this near to the water's-edge. With his eyes as fully adjusted to the darkness as they were ever going to be, Stride was able to maintain a pace along the shoreline that was little slower than any that he could have managed in full daylight and, with Parsons now directly at his heels, he soon came to the clearing that could only be Buckle's farmyard and got a much closer view of the barn-light than the one that he had received earlier from the land to the south of the river. Halting, he advised that they had reached the Buckle property and turned to his left, fetching his horse about; then, as it was obvious that there was nothing further on which they need waste words, Parsons did likewise, and they began retracing their steps eastwards, the deputy sheriff now leading the way.

Before long they were treading ground which they had not covered previously. Stride started to wonder how far this pinewood extended, for chance and distance began to seem at odds. Lulled by the simple exercise of putting one foot in front of the other, he felt his concentration slipping, and there was little tension in him any more. Then, just as he was on the brink of admitting to himself that Parsons and he must somehow have got it wrong from the outset, he heard a voice out of the darkness which sounded so clear and immediate that he believed for a moment the deputy had spoken to him; but in the same instant he realized that he had been deceived by the sound and that the speaker was standing somewhere ahead of him and was in fact one of a small group; for now talk chased back and forth under the trees, seeming oddly weird and isolated in this strange stillness below the wind; and Stride's solar plexus tightened up again and he could have kicked himself for letting his mind become fixed by an earlier supposition that common sense ought long ago to have demolished. For he had accepted that the surviving crooks – with whom there was no doubt that Parsons and he had just made contact – would have loaded their booty on reaching the river and taken to the water at once; but now he saw that on a night as dark as this had become since the moon had been blotted out, such an action could amount to suicide, for the Powder River was obviously no placid stream and must have its fair share of snags, rapids, and sandbanks. There could be no doubt that rafting by night would be feasible under a good moon – and there could be little question that the badmen had done their planning in the expectation of one – but nobody could have foreseen the almost perpetually overcast heavens which April had brought so far.

Stopping his horse – and thankful that Parsons had proved more alert than he and already done the same – Stride turned and walked back along the nearside of his mount's body, reaching out with a hand beyond its tail until he touched the deputy's clothing. 'Sounds to me like there's three or four of them,' he whispered. 'They're standing just a little ahead of us. Figures they daren't take to the river. It's dark out there. I didn't really consider that might hold them back.'

'I think there was some doubt deep in my mind concerning it,' Parsons said. 'Don't you wish we have a posse now?'

'Why, sure,' Stride admitted. 'But we're here now, and can't change how it is. At worst, they're only two to one. How if we try to surround them with a ghost posse? There's a mite of reflection off the surface of the river. If we can position ourselves so that their shapes are even faintly visible against it, we may be able to cut them down if we call on them to surrender and they want to make a fight of it.'

'The advantage of surprise is with us,' Parsons observed. 'There's no telling what the shock of a challenge might do. It's worth a try.'

'You set it out.'

'Let the horses stand here,' Parsons said promptly. 'You go to the further side of them, and I'll stand to landward. That way we'll have them penned after a fashion.'

'Okay,' Stride said. 'But we'll have to be mighty light of foot when we move round back of them. A cracking twig or a rustling bush could be enough to give us away.'

'No need to stress the obvious,' Parsons chided. 'You go first. I'll issue the challenge. Be ready to back me up with your gun or voice when I do.'

'We'll make it seem real,' Stride promised, catfooting away to his left and moving back into the trees as he began making what he judged would be a wide enough curve to take him to the rear of the ground occupied by the unseen crooks and then into a threatening position on the eastern side of them.

Breath bated and setting his feet down with the utmost care, he completed the first half of his semi-arc soundlessly enough, and had entered the second when, on looking up, he saw that a clearing of some size had been made in the riverside timber at this point, and he supposed that it must have been from here that the badmen had chopped down the trees to build the raft which would now be tethered somewhere along the strip of bank nearby.

Believing that he glimpsed the outlaws once – centrally placed and dimly silhouetted against the faint translucence of the river – Stride kept padding through his curve and, as much by luck as any pretence of woodcraft, he arrived in the position that Parsons had indicated for him and halted beside a tree, drawing his Colt and facing into the clearing. Then he stood like a statue and waited for the deputy sheriff to issue the challenge that would almost certainly bring the night to life again, for he could not really believe that the thieves standing yonder – with a crime already committed that could cost them the rest of their lives in jail – were going to give up without making a big fight of it.

Suddenly Stride heard the unmistakable rasping of a Winchester's loading mechanism as it lifted a cartridge into the rifle's barrel; and then the deputy's voice bellowed: 'We've got you surrounded, boys! I have three dozen guns pointing your way! Surrender – or you'll be shot down where you stand!'

'Oh, good grief!' yelped a voice that sounded very like Banker Lambourne's. 'We're done for!'

'Don't talk so damned foolish!' snarled another man, the tones unquestionably those of Dan Wall. 'It's only Ralph Parsons, the deputy sheriff! He can't possibly have formed a posse that size in the time!'

'Oh, yes he can have!' Stride declared, triggering a couple of shots towards the river. 'We've got you where we want you, Wall, and we'll surely kill you if you don't give up right now!'

'Who d'you think you're kidding, Stride?' Wall demanded after a just perceptible hesitation; and after that he fired three fast shots in answer to the pair that had travelled his way. 'Lambourne, Cocklin – get on the raft!'

'No!' Lambourne's voice cried indignantly. 'I'll give the orders, and I say – !'

'You say nothing, fat man!' came Wall's snarl. 'Your part is done! Get on that raft – or I'll blow your head off!'

Stride heard feet start running towards the river-bank from the position that he believed Parsons to have occupied. Cocking his revolver, he also broke into a run and began making for the water's-edge. Then, though he did nothing to acknowledge his awareness of it, Stride first heard and then glimpsed a figure racing away from the side of the river and heading for the trees behind the clearing. There, he was pretty sure – while wondering if Parsons had also picked out the darting presence – was the fourth man whom he was reasonably certain that he had heard among the talking crooks at the start of this episode. The escaper was very important, but there simply wasn't time to chase him now. What mattered was to stop the raft leaving the river's southern shore and getting out into mid-stream where the currents flowed fast.

Yet again Stride found himself cursing the lack of light. Arriving suddenly at the river's brink, he halted almost too late and stood teetering above the water, fighting for his balance as he peered to left and right. It seemed to him in the pressure of his need that he could see nothing but the blackest stripes of shadow on the vague shimmer of the flow, and he felt constrained to once more blast at random – again in the hope of provoking a response that would betray the position of his enemies – when he heard the noises of wood creaking under strain and the humming of an over-stretched rope under tension that was no less great; and then he perceived that beside his right boot was the post to which the raft was undoubtedly secured.

Stride bent towards the rope, intent on taking the floating raft's position from the tug, but he had yet to make up his mind as to where the structure was, when he heard the thud of an axe aboard the raft and the strain went out of the rope as its further end sprang away from whatever point to which it had been moored and splashed into the water, the watcher's narrowed eyes finally picking up the floating platform's position as the current caught the nearer end of it and gave it a slow twirl towards the river's streaming centre.

Letting fly at the dimly discerned raft, Stride heard his bullet hammer into wood. Next instant two revolvers began flashing their replies. Stride sank low as bullets spat above and around him. Coming to rest on his right knee, he sighted and fired again, but just then his target seemed to blink out and he clamped down on his desire to keep shooting, for he had with him only the ammunition which the loops of his gun-belt held and this had already been badly depleted by the day's various demands upon it. Parsons, who had arrived at the waterside moments behind him, sent a few shots after those which Stride had discharged but, though the guns on the raft were no longer answering, it was almost certain that he too failed to hit anything, and he let his Colt fall silent.

'Wall again,' Stride commented flatly, his Colt reeking under his nostrils as he began a reload of its fired chambers. 'He made the difference. Lambourne would have thrown in his hand.'

'We follow,' Parsons said.

'There was a fourth man,' Stride reflected. 'He left, pelting in the opposite direction, as we headed for the river. Did you see him?'

'I saw somebody.'

'At a guess, Deputy, I'd say it was your boss.'

'Mayhap.'

'You'll want to get him.'

'If it was him, aye,' Parsons acknowledged. 'Would he be heading back to Pan Town?'

'What d'you think?'

'If it *was* him, no,' the deputy answered. 'George Hurst has his blind spots, but he's a canny critter and always knows when to cut and run.'

'Now I'll tell you what I think,' Stride said, tossing a handful of spent shells into the water. 'I think Hurst has the job of taking the horses down the river.'

'Why would he do that?' Parsons inquired, sounding at a loss. 'I reckon those evil varmints on the raft have more than wealth enough with them to buy new mounts when they've crossed the line into Nebraska.'

'Sure,' Stride agreed, tipping his Colt back into its holster. 'But that applies to things as they were. Do you still see them leaving the river near Mitchell or Scottsbluff? I don't. And that means they're going to need their horses to pack that gold again. They've been found out, and they'll recognise the risk that we could use the telegraph to alert the Federal law for hundreds of miles around. That's why I'm sure they'll leave the river far short of where they originally intended. They may even do it while they're still in Wyoming. However it's done, they'll need the horses to carry the gold.'

'I will say this for you, Stride,' Parsons said with a note of quiet admiration in his voice, 'I'd rather have you with me than against me. I'll get after the man with the horses. You can follow the raft down the river.'

'Very good,' Stride said. 'You watch out. It's George Hurst all right, and you be wary of him. He'll have a crafty eye to his back trail, and a bullet for the man on it.'

'Same goes for you,' Parsons cautioned. 'There are three of them. It wouldn't surprise me if they put one ashore with orders to despatch you for your harp.'

'I'll be watching,' Stride assured him. 'Let's get our horses and split.'

They walked back along the bank of the river to where they had left their mounts. Then, with a word of farewell, they parted. Parsons walked his horse southwards into the trees, while Stride resumed what had become a familiar plodding along the bank of the river. The water rushed and swirled and the wind moaned, but the sounds amounted to a form of company, and Stride felt suddenly bereft as he passed out of the trees and found himself unprotected where the rain settled coldly on his brow and the chasing airs stirred the hair on his nape.

But there was some compensation for this abrupt exposure. Away from the danger of low-hanging boughs, he could ride his horse again, and this he did, but always keeping his sixth sense active and seeking the tiniest vibration of menace from anywhere in the night's dismal vault. Thus the hours came and went – and periods of rain and moonshine with them – but never once did Stride feel seriously endangered, for his common sense told him that with the night so inclement and the problems of navigating what must be a large raft on a difficult river so great, it was unlikely that anybody would attempt to come ashore and lay for him before daylight.

The small hours lengthened towards the dawn, and Stride began to feel very tired. His sleep during the previous night had been uneasy, and his rest during the day had never been free from anxiety. Add this to his intense activity since escaping from the Pan Town jailhouse and it wasn't so surprising that he should be starting to feel sapped in both body and mind. His horse, too, was drooping, and there came the temptation to steal a rest, but he knew that the crooks, with the water under them, could not and would not rest, and that, if fortune had not deserted them, they must be getting further and further ahead all the time. Indeed, there were moments when, considered logically, pursuing the raft seemed a waste of effort; but, short of giving up, there was nothing else for it; and at the back of everything was the instinctive recognition that Providence was the final arbiter and that more things could go wrong for the badmen than were likely to go wrong for him.

As if Nature had been shamed by the quality of recent days, sunup revealed skies blown clear; and Stride, more than half asleep in his saddle, found most things largely out of drawing in the grey emptiness of the hour. He kept reaching after purpose and a new grasp on the deadly facts of his situation, but tiredness numbed all and there loomed an added danger – unbelievable in a normal state of rest – of ceasing to care. Then from one extreme of consciousness he was snatched violently to the other; for the crash of a rifle shocked him instantly awake in every aspect of his being. Stiffening in his saddle, he glanced slightly to the southwest of him – where the echoes were rolling – and felt a cold hand close on his heart and squeeze it almost to a stop.

Parsons? Had the man just died? Was he alone in this now?

TEN

The questions were clearly unanswerable and, flinging off his dread, Stride swore at himself in a comprehensive fashion. While there could be no denying the probability that the shot which he had just heard had concerned the deputy sheriff and the man whom Parsons was pursuing, it could as easily have been fired by the lawman himself as George Hurst, whom Stride presumed to have charge of the horses belonging to the outlaws. And, of course, there was also the outside chance that the detonation had come from somebody out shooting for the pot. The hour was right.

Reassured by this somewhat illusory thinking – if still disturbed in his emotions – Stride kept making such small adjustments as the terrain forced on him and moving with the river. The majesty of the country loomed at him in a vastness of contour that grew ever more black-etched as colour returned to the east and radiant fingers of pale fire burnished the skyline above the rising sun. Then, as rock bore Stride upwards and the nearby river cut deep into a canyon, blue washed into the morning sky and acquired a touch of iridescence, all the promise of the new season seeming to clothe the distant ridges in a pearly glow. Stride's blood felt the rising Spring. Once more his body was filled with youth, and his mind was clear and purposeful.

But if Stride responded thus to the influences of the April morning, his horse did not and, arriving on the rimrock, he felt obliged to dismount and lead the flagging brute along the canyon's southern lip. On his left the rock fell grey and sheer for hundreds of feet, and the river flowed darkly at its foot. As before, Stride felt at the mercy of powers over which he had no control, and his sense of isolation increased his awareness that he had not the slightest idea where his quarry might be on the waters beneath.

He looked helplessly ahead and to his rear. Wall and company could by now be steering a steady course down the middle of the flow many a mile ahead, they could have come ashore for breakfast, or they could even have grounded long miles back and be wading among the stones of a fleet bottom in some willow-bound section of the river where a passing eye would fail to penetrate. Experienced as he was, he was sure about one thing – his new lease of life would not last beyond midday; and his horse would have to be rested long before then; so he could have all manner of decisions to make in the next few hours and might even do well to abandon his arm of the chase along the Powder River and seek to find out whether Ralph Parsons was still okay. If the deputy sheriff had fallen victim to ambush, he could try to tack on behind the man responsible and stealthily take over that aspect of the pursuit. He ought to be able to follow the horse-minder to whatever rendezvous had been agreed between the man and his confederates on the raft and perhaps position himself to some advantage for a showdown. Indeed, now he came to give the matter his full mind, he was sure that that would prove the wiser course; for, once he had tracks to follow, he could rest when necessary and thus reduce the fatigue that he and his horse were already feeling. More, whatever the length of the chase, he would be sure that it would have a definite conclusion and not peter out into the kind of aimless failure that he seemed to be contemplating at present.

Pausing, abruptly confirmed in this new course, Stride looked downwards and to the south of him, intending to leave the rimrock here and now and descend into the part of the lower country that he expected the horse-minder to be crossing at this time, but he saw at once that the slopes he was now contemplating were much too steep and treacherous to permit such a descent, and he found himself left with the choice of going on or going back. If he went back, his downward climb would return him to the area in which he had earlier heard the rifle shot – which could be a help in the possible search for Parsons' body – but if the tracks that he hoped to quickly run across should show that to be unnecessary, he would be placing himself far to the horse-minder's rear, without any need, and have all that catching up to do. If he went on, he would of course be gambling to some extent against discovering the need to go back, but he must eventually come to a spot from which descent would be easy, and his retained advantage of height until that time possibly give him a glimpse of the horse-minder – and even Parsons – on the fairly open land to the south of him.

Deciding to go on, he resumed walking the rimrock, his horse drooping at his heels, and he had covered about another mile and spotted the right-hand bend beyond which the canyon appeared to terminate when, just into the curve – where sand cast up when the waters were in spate had banked in considerable quantities – he spotted signs of movement and, as he got closer, perceived that he was gazing down on the grounded raft and the rope-assisted efforts which the three men with it were making to drag it clear of the sticking point.

Stride felt a moment of satisfaction and relief. There they were – Wall, Lambourne, and Denny Cocklin. The sight proved that they had been ahead of him by some bit, but now they had lost their lead and he doubted that they were going any further; for he could already discern their predicament and knew that greed would not allow them to remedy it. As he judged it, the recent rains had caused more water than was normal for the time of year to flow through the narrows down there, and the forces of the initial cataract had literally picked the craft up and sent it sliding across the surface until it had gone aground. Stride knew that his observations might not be totally accurate from this distance, but he was fairly certain that if the raft were substantially unloaded the united strength of the three men on the ropes would be sufficient to haul it back into the river; but, with this need unmet – and allowing for the crooks' undoubted fear that once their craft was off the sandbank the currents would take over and sweep it beyond all hope of reloading – it appeared to the watcher that the trio could tug for everlasting and not shift the raft an inch.

Well, their folly was his gain, for he could see a place not far ahead where he was sure that he could descend the no longer vertical southern wall of the canyon – using its ledges, acclivities, chimneys and such – and arrive on the narrow bank which had lately appeared on this side of the river and offered a place from which to challenge the three men below where it bulged towards the sandbank and the floating platform trapped there.

Realizing that one of the crooks need only look up and round and he would be seen as surely as he could see, Stride picked out a spot on the slope behind the rimrock and led his horse to it. He ground-tied the animal; then, scrambling back to the capstone's broad parade, he walked on several paces more and came to the section of the canyon wall down which he planned to make his descent.

Kneeling, he spied once more on the scene below; then, satisfied that the three crooks were still engrossed in their task and had no interest in the bluff opposite them, he turned his legs over the rimrock and lowered himself slowly into a chimney with a saw-toothed pattern of erosion down its back. Using the sawteeth as he might have done a ladder, Stride climbed downwards for the fifty feet of the chimney's length, then backed out onto a boulder-studded slope that took him down another hundred and more. After that, hanging down from a ledge, he dropped about fifteen feet onto the first of six terraces – had a few dangerous moments passing from one to another of these – and a much easier time sitting on his heels and slithering down a lower slope, completing his descent by easing himself through a fissure that had been partially choked by the debris from a run-off and stepping out onto the shoreline itself, the three men and their stuck raft now so close across the intervening thirty feet of water that he could hear their words of advice to each other and even the heaviness of their breathing as they put out all their strength time and again.

Stride drew his revolver and pointed it towards the sandbank, cocking it as he called: 'Put your hands in the air, gents, and let's have no nonsense!'

The three crooks stopped work abruptly. Their faces came round, but the expressions on them were more questioning than startled. Then their essential bewilderment gave place to rage as they fully digested that they were being challenged by an enemy whom they had obviously not expected to see. Denny Cocklin began to stamp around in the water like a madman, Banker Lambourne wrung his hands and looked close to tears, but Dan Wall, after an instant of murderous snarling, broke into a grin and revealed himself the supreme optimist by shouting: 'Glad to see you, Mr Stride! Put that gun away before you do yourself a mischief! Swim over here, son, and lay hand to one of these ropes! Why spite yourself, man? We ain't greedy pigs! There's gold enough on our raft to give you years and years of happy life!' His right arm beckoned. 'Come on then!'

'Oh, go to hell, Daniel!' Stride retorted. 'You're worse than toothache! Get your hands up!'

Wall lifted his hands into the air. 'Now what? I can't swim. Some of the water between you and me is deep enough to drown a house. Are you expecting me to walk over to you?'

'Not at all your style!' Stride agreed ironically. 'Swim – or drown. I don't give a damn. Just get your butt over here!'

'Isn't that like you!' Wall complained. 'Don't be such a sourpuss! We're miles from anywhere, Stride. You can do what you like, and there's nobody but us to see. This river doesn't know ass from ass-upwards. You're never going to have another chance like this!'

'An even share, Mr Stride!' Lambourne promised unctuously. 'Make your home in Washington D.C., escort the prettiest woman, enjoy the richest foods, sail the world. It's all waiting for you!'

'Get ye back to the burning, mister!' Stride advised. 'That's your ideal – not mine!'

'God damn you then!' Wall shouted, making the fastest draw that the man on the riverbank opposite him had ever seen, but missing by a foot with his shot.

Stride fired back. Wall flung wide his arms and fell

back against the sandbank which held the raft fast. He hung there, like one crucified, his cheeks grey, mouth pursed and fishlike, and eyes partially glazed. He looked in a very poor way – though Stride could see no blood upon his body – and his gun fell out of his relaxing fingers and slipped under the surface of the river.

'I won't be took!' Denny Cocklin bawled, jerking his Colt and firing across the water.

Feeling a tiny wind as the bullet passed his left ear, Stride aimed his own gun at the centre of Cocklin's chest and squeezed the trigger. He saw the shirt twitch over the badman's heart, and Cocklin buckled up and wallowed slackly at the edge of a current's swirl, his frame sinking slowly as it spiralled away downstream, only the grey of his hair showing as a shadow of blood spread darkly in his wake.

Stride believed that the finish of it. He could not imagine that the banker would try it. Suddenly, however, a twin-barrelled derringer jumped into his right hand from a sleeve spring. The little weapon flashed, but it was a forty-five calibre slug that burned a furrow across Stride's left forearm.

Angered by the pain, Stride fired on the banker. Lambourne heaved together, shuddering, and looked afraid. Nevertheless, he thumbed clumsily at his tiny gun and clearly meant to shoot a second time. Forced to it, Stride stamped his feet apart and fanned his Colt empty, the bullets ripping up the front of the banker's once immaculate lawn shirt, and Lambourne faced round with a certain unnatural grace and collapsed over the corner of the raft nearest to him and lay there, unquestionably dead.

Lowering his gun, Stride experienced a moment of self-revulsion. He had killed men, and found it easy. Could he have done differently here? Life – even that of a villainous kind – suddenly seemed all-important. What if he had fired to wound? Yet how could he have risked that? The gun game was played for keeps, and it depended on the split second. Self-preservation was the first law of Nature, and one that even the most civilised of men obeyed implicitly. It had been kill or be killed – and he had killed. There had been no more evil in it than that.

Surely now it was all over? But then he realized that the question itself had been prompted by the awareness that something was not as it should be. What had become of Dan Wall? The man's upper body was no longer spread cruciform against the sandbank. In fact the gunman had disappeared altogether. What the – ?

Instinctively, Stride threw a glance downstream. He saw no trace of the badman at first, but then glimpsed a human shape a yard beneath the surface that was swimming with just enough strength to use the current to the best advantage while staying submerged. And then it came to him that Wall had not even been wounded. His bullet must have struck the big steel buckle at the front of his enemy's gunbelt and been deflected. No wonder there had been no blood on Wall's torso and he had resembled a landed fish. He had simply been winded.

Well, Dan'l might figure himself no end smart, but

he wasn't going to get away – and neither was he going to die of a swift and painless bullet. No, sir! Dan'l Wall was going to stand on the drop, with the executioner's black hood blinding him and the rope tight beneath his chin. He was going to hear the crowd singing 'We will gather at the River' with all their dreadful enthusiasm, and the parson gabbling that last prayer. Dan'l was going to plunge into hell through the scarlet flash of his severing spine, and in that final instant he was going to understand that the horror of his death was no more than fit payment for his callous murder of Sandra Aves. But first Wall was going to get another hiding – one that would keep his lying tongue quiet all the way back to Pan Town!

Holstering his empty Colt, Stride turned to his right and began trotting along the waterside. He watched the river growing shallower as it spread beyond the narrows of the bend and began straightening into the continuation of its journey towards the Platte. Content to await the right moment for his plunge after the swimmer, Stride let Wall come up for air a couple of times and dive again in the belief that his escape was going ahead successfully. Then, as the river completely cleared the canyon and was briefly sliced up into a number of courses by slim green eyots and grey pebble beds of a similar shape, he waded thigh-deep into the water and seized Wall by the collar, dragging his torso upwards until he was compelled to touch bottom with his soles and once more support himself in the vertical position.

The big man spat and spluttered. He screwed to the

right, eyes hating as they met Strides, and he hit out with both fists, but the pebbles under his feet provided unstable footing and he reeled awkwardly from the force of his own leverage, his punches going round either side of Stride's body. Stride, more firmly placed, hooked at the solar plexus with his right and crossed a left to the chin, bringing both fists down on the gunman's nape as Wall folded up; but, desperate as he was, the big man fought his collapse and willed his recovery, the effort in the wrenched lines of his face as he butted for his opponent's jaw with the top of his head and drove punches into either side of Stride's belly.

Stride staggered, but wasn't hurt – except in so far as the water stung his nicked forearm and the slight bullet-graze to the body that he had received at the battle of the waggon during the previous evening – and he promptly blocked the blows with which Wall followed up, then hauled back and, gathering his inner forces, whipped over a succession of punches to the head that carried all his weight and strength and totally scrambled the big man's senses. Slack-kneed and glassy-eyed, Wall reeled and splashed about, sitting down and wobbling up, and it would have been easy to bruise and cut him to ribbons; but, with the other at his mercy, Stride perceived that he had done damage enough and that brutality for its own sake would only reduce him to the level of the type of man that he had always despised. So, steadying Wall from the belt, he turned him round and gave him a shove towards the shore, adding further pushes as he pursued the gunman's punch-drunken course out of the water; but he did no more than look on as Wall reached the water's-edge and went sprawling on his face in the dirt and shingle beyond.

Breathing hard himself, Stride gave it a few moments, then closed slowly on the prostrate gunman, squeezing some of the water out of his sodden trousers as he went; and, in what proved his faulty belief that the conscious malice had all been thrashed out of the big man, he almost ceased watching for threatening movements in him; but he just had time to recognise what the sudden groping of the hand at the top of his enemy's right boot was all about, and he swiftly lunged forward and down, robbing the other of the stiletto that was sheathed and hidden there. 'Hard luck, Daniel,' he said, retreating again and thrusting the needle-pointed dagger into the back of his own belt. 'You're all out of kilter this morning, aren't you?'

'May you rot, Stride!' Wall coughed out, trying to force himself off the ground but failing.

'I know,' Stride soothed, still full of his mocking sympathy. 'It sure is hard, Daniel. How'd it happen, hey? Beaten silly again by a guy you're sure is worthless.' Then he seized the back of the other's collar with both hands and yanked upwards with all his strength. 'Upsy-daisy!'

'Hell-and-dammit!' Wall choked. 'May you – !'

'Give it time,' Stride urged, steadying the gunman at the shoulders and pointing him ahead. 'We all rot, boy. Maybe it's the final measure of how much we matter. But the rotting gets done by hanged killers sooner than it does by most folk.' Once more he laid a hand between Wall's shoulder-blades and gave him a push. 'Let's go find my horse, shall we? He's up on the rimrock, and it looks to me as if we can reach him from that slope on our right.'

Wall went lurching up the shore, and Stride moved after him. Ahead of them now, and separating them from the more general level of the land around, was a low and slightly undermined bank that was lined with greasewood and chaparral. All appeared still, and the growth looked innocent enough; but then, just before they reached the thickets, there was a stirring in the brush opposite them and George Hurst's figure came breasting into view, the Colt forty-five in his right hand covering them both. 'Hold it, boys!' he warned. 'That *does* mean you too, Dan.'

'What's the game, George?' Wall asked, his tones startled despite their thickness. 'Shoot him, and let's make tracks!'

'I think you're missing the point, Wall,' Stride said grimly. 'If I've got it figured right, the sheriff has been watching us and carefully summing things up. He means to gun us *both* down. You ought to know better than to trust a sheriff; especially one nobody can trust.'

'The gold's safe, George,' Wall persisted, 'and you've got the horses.'

'You've said it,' Hurst agreed. '*One* man, lots of gold, and enough horses. Nice combination.'

Wall straightened his back. It was a matter of insistence rather than persistence with him now. 'The raft is stuck on a sandbank, George,' he said. 'There's a river between you and that gold. You may have your gifts, but can you swim with a hundred pounds of ore on your back?'

'No, Dan,' Hurst admitted, his grin taunting, 'but my horse can.'

'You're going to need help, mister.'

'Not to help myself, Dan.'

'Hell's curse on you, George!' Wall yelled, his restraint dissolving into madness, and he sprang to the front and upwards, his hands reaching for the renegade lawman's ankles; but Hurst's revolver boomed long before the big man's fingers could settle on him, and Wall fetched up abruptly in his tracks, clutching at his chest and screaming thinly. Then he toppled over backwards and came to rest on the earth under the bank, his eyes staring blankly at the sky and his crooked fingers straightening convulsively.

Stride knew that he had a single moment in which to act. Whipping out the stiletto which he had thrust into the back of his belt, he held it across the middle of his right palm with a locking thumb, point to the fore; then, while Hurst was re-cocking his weapon and shifting his aim, swept it at the turncoat lawman. The thin-bladed dagger crossed the intervening space like a silver flash and drove its point deep into Hurst's chest. The renegade sheriff gave a lurch, shooting high as his right arm jerked upwards, then came pitching to the front again, struggling to thumb back his hammer for another shot; but blood suddenly spilled through his teeth and the revolver fell out of nerveless fingers, Hurst pitching off the bank and thudding to rest in a prone position close to where Wall lay.

Going to the man, Stride turned him onto his back. He saw that Hurst was still alive, though obviously fading fast. 'Parsons?' he asked.

Hurst's lips twisted just perceptibly in a sneering refusal.

'It can't matter to you now,' Stride reminded.

'Ralph was always too trusting,' Hurst muttered. 'I stood there and – and he came towards me. I – I shot him, but I don't think I – I killed him. I saw him – him move after he hit the ground. I ought to have gone over and – and finished him off, but – but I had to – ' That was as far as he got, for a shudder travelled through him from head to toe and he died.

'Had to,' Stride said harshly to the newly dead man. 'You had to do nothing. None of you did.'

Then, shaking his head, he left the bodies lying and climbed the bank, eyes upon the rim of the canyon.

ELEVEN

Stride stood checking his horse outside Sadie Aitken's boarding house. He was about to leave Pan Town and, though he had just spent a month in the place – and been praised and well-treated by its people for his doings – he had no twinge of regret. Even blessed by the brightest of Spring days, Pan Town was a cheerless hole and he doubted that anything he might find here could ever make it home. True, he had been a mite prejudiced from the start, but then he was a cowboy, and cowboys were just naturally prejudiced against everything that didn't grow horns, have four hooves, stink to high heaven, and reach a good price in the Chicago beef market.

Mounting up, Stride waved farewell to the several faces watching him out of nearby windows, and then jogged off down the street, thinking with pleasure on the fact that Ralph Parsons, shot through the left lung by George Hurst – but likely to see ninety-two for all that – was now back on his feet and going to make Pan Town a good sheriff. He had said his 'goodbyes' to Ralph last night, and saw no point in stopping at the man's house again; but there was Hetty Gage. He ought to just look in at Jake's Palace and wish Hetty all the best before putting this place and the failure that it represented behind him. For whatever he might have succeeded in, he had come to find and ask a favour of "Pecos Joe" Ralston, and he had ended up doing no better than look down on the man's dead face.

He kept riding southwards along the main street until he came to Jake's Palace. Here he drew rein, swung down again, and hitched his mount. Then he climbed the front steps and entered the building, where he was surprised by the morning hush and the sight of blonde Hetty smoking a stogie and adding stitches to a piece of knitting that had a yoke big enough to fit a buffalo. 'Why, if it ain't old handsome, our very own hero!' the blonde jeered, squinting through a smoke ring. 'Hear you're planning to light a shuck, Billy.'

'You hear right, Hetty,' Stride acknowledged. 'Just off. Got to get back to Denver.'

The blonde nodded mechanically. 'Two plain, one pearl, and twist,' she muttered, adding a choice cuss-word. 'Now look what you've made me do! I've dropped a stitch.'

'Hetty, my dear,' Stride informed her gravely, 'was I you, I'd drop the lot. That's a fearsome strain you're putting on your mind. Have a drink instead.' He shoved a ten dollar gold piece across the bar. 'Buy all the girls a drink, eh? I've been grateful to you all. I was up to my elbows that day until you all came along and got me out of the hoosegow. None of what's happened to me since could have been if it hadn't been for that.'

'As to that,' Hetty said, smiling her thanks as she picked up the Eagle and put it into a china cup on the backbar, 'it made a nice change from routine. It broke the monotony. Life gets tedious for us girls. Would you credit that?'

'Why, surely,' Stride replied. 'Never was a job in the whole of Creation that didn't bore the folks who have to do it sometime. It's what moves us on, I guess. I'd like to see you move on, friend Gage.'

'I've burned all,' Hetty said wryly. 'Nowhere else for me to go – 'cept prison.'

'Many a true word spoken in jest,' Stride conceded, pulling a long face. 'Poor old Orville. That brother of mine will be white-haired by the time they release him from jail. Damn that "Pecos Joe"!'

'Excuse me, sir,' a male voice said.

Stride glanced to his left to find out who had stepped up to his elbow. 'By thunder, you're respectful today, Mr Burridge,' he observed, seeing the goggle-eyed Gandy standing there, matchstick-limbed and deceptively dull-looking in his scaly, monumental ugliness. 'A beer for Mr Burridge, Hetty.'

Burrage opened a newspaper and placed it on the bar; then pushed it under Stride's nose, indicating a few inches of print at the bottom of the third column on page two with a tapping index finger. 'Read that, sir.'

Looking down at the lines, Stride began to read

them aloud, and they went thus:

Yesterday, May tenth, released from Denver Prison, one Orville Stride. Mr Stride had been sentenced to a long stay behind prison walls for what was believed to have been his part in robbing the Columbia and South Colorado Bank at Durango during late October of last year.

Territorial Governor, John James, has quashed Mr Stride's sentence after studying the confessions made by the members of the Thomas O'Henry gang, lately taken in highway robbery. O'Henry and his confederates have admitted to the Durango bank theft, and declared to a man that Orville Stride had no part whatsoever in the crime and was at that time completely unknown to them.

It is understood at the offices of the Denver Mercury that Mr Stride is to be compensated by the Territory of Colorado in the sum of five hundred dollars for wrongful imprisonment. The Mercury would like to endorse the magnanimity of our rulers to the tune of a further one hundred dollars and wish Mr Stride God Speed.

'Would you believe it?' Stride asked, looking heavenwards. 'There's me been through all this, and old Orv is set free with a bonus and a blessing!'

'Isn't that what you wanted?' Burridge asked, saluting with the mug of beer which Hetty had just drawn for him.

'Why, yes,' Stride replied. 'But it would have happened anyhow.'

'You certain of that? Maybe you were needed here.'

'You weren't much help to start with,' Stride accused.

'How do you know what I was?' Burridge challenged.

What could a man say to that? Did even a cowboy know the ends he served? At least he had proved his willingness to be the tool of justice. He ought to be celebrating. Brother Orville had been free this last week, and you could be sure that he had already made a nice hole in those six hundred dollars. Stride reckoned he'd get drunk; but then he decided to stay sober. Drunks got too close to the truth, and he felt somehow that he had had enough of that for one day. 'I thank you for the lesson in – I know not what, Mr Burridge,' he said, slapping a silver dollar on the divide. 'Kindly drink that up, sir, and fare-you-well, Miss Gage.'

'So long, Bill,' the woman said. 'Don't look for answers. There ain't any. Good luck.'

Stride turned away from the bar and, lifting a hand, walked out of Jake's Palace. All was well in his world again, yet he felt cheated. He suspected that Hetty Gage had got it right. It was no good looking for answers. There weren't any. You simply did what you had to do the best way you could. If it worked out to your satisfaction, fine. If it didn't – you went home to Colorado.

zen

meditations

on being a true friend

richard craze
zen
meditations
on being a true friend

introduction

Without friends we are alone in the world. A friend is someone with whom we can be ourselves, whom we can share with and laugh with, and whom we can turn to when the world grows cold.

Friendship sweetens life, it makes the good times better, and the bad times easier to bear. And yet it is all too easy to take a friend for granted, to fail to realize what we have until we lose it. Friendship is a gift, but not one that should be treated lightly, it must be treasured, looked after, endlessly renewed and nurtured.

This little book of meditations celebrates the joy of friendship, and provides the perfect opportunity to spend a little time thinking about friends, past and present. It encourages contemplation and appreciation of friendship, in a world which is often too busy and hectic to allow quiet thought. To accompany the meditations there is a CD of music which has been specially composed to reflect the varied moods of friendship and to ease contemplation. Take a few minutes out of your day to dwell on some of the meditations, and through this time thinking about the value of friendship, you will find the energy to strengthen and regenerate those relationships that are important to you. The music can be used in conjunction with the meditations, or alone as a tool to aid relaxation.

the call of a friend

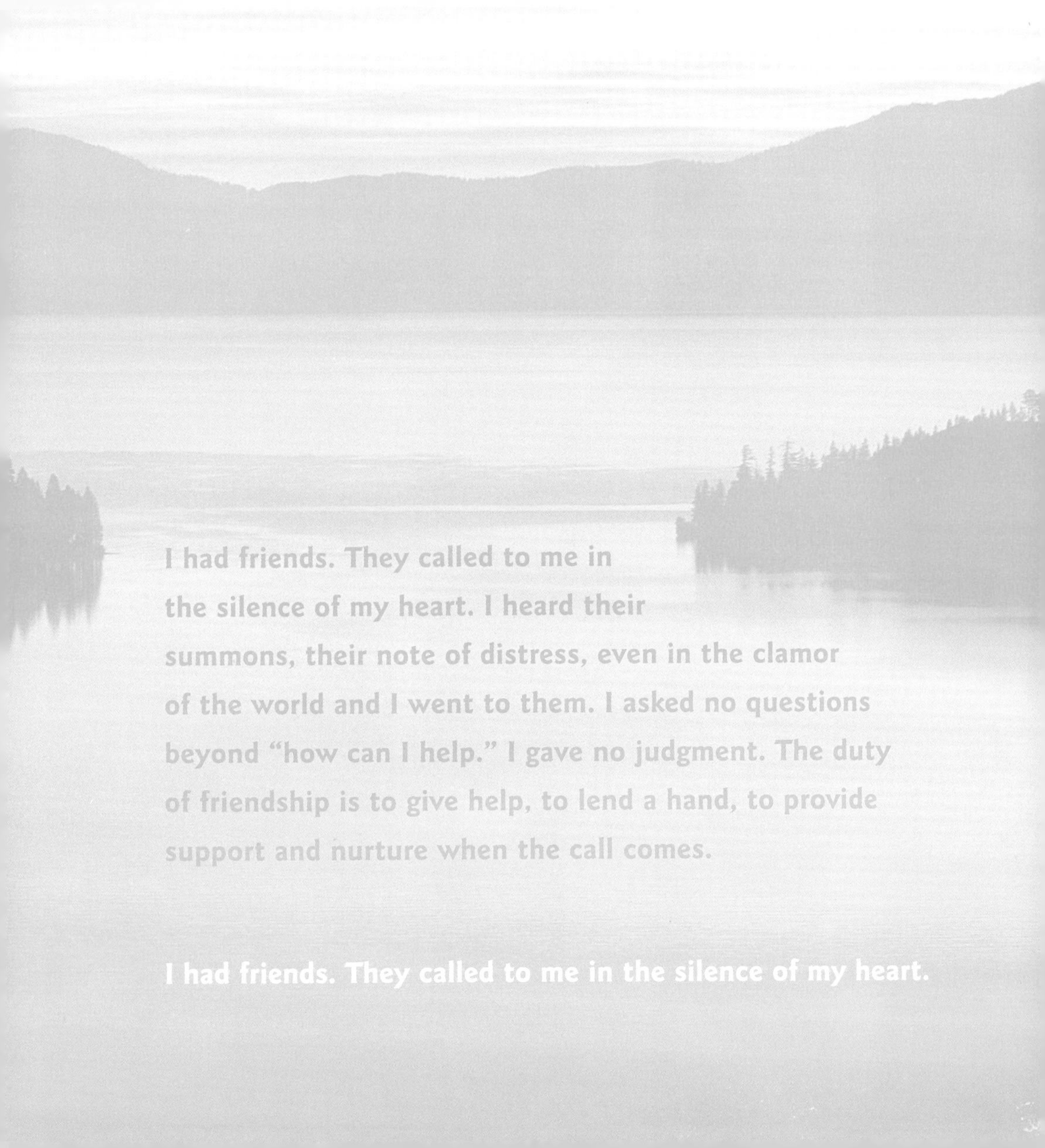

I had friends. They called to me in the silence of my heart. I heard their summons, their note of distress, even in the clamor of the world and I went to them. I asked no questions beyond "how can I help." I gave no judgment. The duty of friendship is to give help, to lend a hand, to provide support and nurture when the call comes.

I had friends. They called to me in the silence of my heart.

true friends

A very long time ago in Japan there were two friends. One played a stringed instrument and the other listened. They both performed their role equally skillfully. When the musician played a tune about mountains or water the listener would say, "I can see mountains," or, "I can hear the running water."

The listener grew old and died, and the musician cut the strings of his instrument—never to play again. Since then the cutting of strings has always been a Zen sign of intimate friendship.

choice of friends

Friendship isn't like going to the library and borrowing a novel on a casual basis. Friendship is more like nurturing and caring for an old book; dusting it off; rereading it with love and care. We may know the story, the order of the words, the chapter titles, and even the ending, but we still derive enormous pleasure from the way the book is put together. So it is with friendship.

We know our friends' gestures and responses, expressions and moods, but we still derive satisfaction from being in their company time and time again.

A true friend is like a very rare and valuable book.

you are

The world turned its back on me but you didn't.
The world thought me a fool but you didn't.
The world laughed at me, you didn't.

my friend

When everyone else walked out you walked in. When everyone else deserted me you were there to pick me up. When everything was dark and unbending you were there with light and comfort. When I thought I had reached the end of the road you urged me on another mile. When there was no hope you brought it. When there was confusion you brought clarity. And when there were good times again you were there to share them with me. You are my friend.

by my side

I don't need a leader to follow. I don't need a follower to trail in my footsteps. I don't need a support or a crutch. I don't need a victim or someone to rescue. I need a friend to walk by my side and be a companion.

what is a friend?

A friend is
someone who
comes when
you need them.

When you are ill they plump up your pillows, make tea, bring flowers, and let you talk until you feel sleepy.

And then
they quietly
slip away
without
waking you
to say
good-bye.

remembering good friends

I count myself in nothing else so happy

When we look back, will it be the money we have made and spent that we remember? The loves won and lost? Or the good friends that we have made and still have by us? Good friends love us unconditionally and cannot be frittered away like money. Good friends won't desert us for another lover, friendship is not exclusive, it can be shared and, in doing so, grows in our love.

As in a soul remembering my good friends

Richard II, William Shakespeare

Friendship is like a plant. In the early stages we have to water and nurture it. As it grows we take pleasure from its increasing strength. And when it finally comes to bloom, it repays all our endeavors and we delight in its colors, its fragrant scent, and its beauty. And friendship, like a flower, will have its seasons. When the petals of friendship drop away we know it is only a passing time, and come the spring it will return and we will welcome it back with renewed enthusiasm and love.

nurturing friendships

I love everything that's old; old friends,
old times, old manners, old books, old wines.
She Stoops to Conquer, Oliver Goldsmith

old friends

A true friendship, like a fine wine, will only improve with age. It grows heady with taste, intoxicating with richness, and gains in value. But unlike a fine wine it cannot be completely emptied; no matter how much we drink of it, there is always more to pour. An old friendship is something to be savored, it doesn't go out of favor or fashion. It is one of the greatest riches of life.

There is
an old
Chinese
saying: Spend old money on new friends, new money on old friends—and if you truly want to honor a friend write their name on the wings of a dragon. If you want to honor a friend then the idea of a dragon

on the wings of a

soaring in splendor with your friend's name written on its wing is a fine and noble vision indeed. How could you not want to honor your friends? How could you achieve this in a dragonless age?

dragon

the smallness of friendship

Friendship is a small thing. It cannot be bought, sold, bartered or traded, it costs nothing. It cannot be manufactured, designed or updated. It cannot be measured or weighed, nor can its volume be found. It doesn't require you to fall in love as a relationship does, but it does contain an element of love. It doesn't require unending sacrifice as having a family does, but it contains elements of family within it. It can stand long periods apart and still be strong. It can suffer arguments and disagreements and still be enduring. It is a small thing, friendship, but the world would be much smaller without it.

a rejoicing of friendship

When I fail, my friends cheer me up, dust me off and set me back on the path. They take no delight in my downfall as my enemies do. When I succeed they rejoice with me. They are not jealous. They do not temper my joy with criticism or advice. They are simply happy to share my triumphs without taking anything away from my moment. They never expect too much of me, and my failures make no difference to them. They give me support, help, comfort and, most importantly, are just there where I know they will be.

the non-mask of friendship

With my lover I have to wear a mask, we all do. We strut, and pretend, and declare our love but never truly reveal all of ourselves. We all do this and it is necessary to maintain the illusion. But with my friends I can strip away the mask and be myself. I have nothing to gain by pretending anything, and they would see through my attempts.

With my friends I can be the real me. I can dare to be myself.

defining friendship

The word friend comes form the Old English "frëond" which means "free."

A friend is someone who sets you free. Allows you to be free. Gives you the freedom and space to be yourself. Doesn't hem you in or impose restrictions. A friend allows you to settle, to be relaxed, and just to be. A friend is the gateway to freedom.

a friend is someone who lies to you

Thank heavens we have friends, for they are the ones who will lie to us. When they've seen our ex-lover they'll tell us how unhappy they looked. When we have failed they will tell us what a marvelous opportunity we've just created for growth and learning. When we wear something totally unsuitable they will tell us how good we look. When we need to lose weight they will tell us cuddly is in. They are the ones who tell us those little white lies no one else would dare to—and they are the ones we know are lying and we love them for it as it is done without malice or judgment.

Life is a bit of bread and butter. That's all we have. Some of us have a little less butter and some of us have stale bread. But we all have a little bit of bread and butter.

A friendship is something that puts a little bit of honey on the bread and butter of life. We can survive without it, but it certainly sweetens our way.

a little honey

filling in the silences

In all conversations there are silences-those little pauses where nothing gets said. In some conversations there is a need to fill those silences, to jump in with further gossip or chat. But a friendship is one place where those silences don't have to be filled. A friendship is somewhere where you can relax and allow that silence to speak volumes all of its own about the need for privacy and space and freedom. Somewhere where you are both content to take a breather from life and just sit and be; to enjoy each other's company without having to speak. Friendship fills the silence without words.

Imagine the world full of darkness. A lover can illuminate the gloom with brief flashes of joy, and the birth of a child is a steady beam of hope. A friend doesn't bring light but a hand to hold in the darkness for comfort. A friend isn't there to lead or guide you through the dark, but to walk by your side in equality and balance. A friend is there to share the darkness and not to offer advice or help about how to dispel the dim mystery of life.

A friend is there to walk with you in the darkness and stumble with you and to make you laugh at your fear of the dark.

a friend in the dark

reserved for friends

Your heart is big enough to hold many people—lovers, children, partners, parents, and family. But there is a special place within your heart that is reserved for a very few special friends. That space cannot be filled with anyone else. That space has a permanent "reserved" sign on it that cannot be moved aside to make room for anyone but close friends. And until that space is filled your heart will always seem half empty.

It is better to have one true friend than hundreds of acquaintances. Friendship takes time and care to develop, it needs nurturing and protecting. It is as difficult to have a huge number of "intimate friends" as it is to juggle with thirty balls and keep them all in the air at the same time.

one true friend

True happiness consists not in
the multitude of friends,
But in the worth and choice.

Ben Jonson

musical friends

I see myself as a musical note. I vibrate like a stringed instrument. My friends also make a similar sound—but different from mine. Together we make music. When we play together we have a harmony. With different friends I play different music. There is no competition. Sometimes I like to play soft and slow, and at other times loud and fast. I need different friends for different concerts, to create different moods and music. My friends are my symphony, my chorus, my melody.

I have a friend. She turns up when she wants, never when she says she will. She is

I have a friend

unreliable,
late,
irresponsible,
embarrassing,
loud,
uncouth,
and wild.
I have a friend. I love her because
she is everything I yearn to be
and everything I dare not be.

the word

We have one word for love—love. We have to use this word for the way we feel about our partner, children, family, parents, and friends. But this word has so many different meanings that when we say we love our friends we cannot express exactly what we mean. The word isn't big enough or grand enough to cover what we feel. We can say we love you in forgiveness, in comfort, in acceptance, in sharing, and in joy.

for love

The word love isn't enough but it is all we have and we need to say it more.

losing friends

To maintain our friendships we have to service them, make repairs, give them a lick of paint, have them regularly checked for faults and the beginnings of problems. We have to make an effort or they fall into disrepair. We have to be the first to cross the street.

In every friend we lose a part of ourselves, and the best part.

Alexander Pope, *Letters*. 1714

the best part of

friendship

It is true we lose a part of ourselves in every friend—but they also lose a part of themselves in us. It is an exchange, a mutual giving where they open their heart to us, and we to them. We can then give and take the best part and replace it with our own. By this collective replacement we both grow and improve until we are able to give to other friends—and so it goes on. Each giving and taking, each growing and expanding in love and affection.

the mathematics of friendship

Friendships have a curious mathematics all of their own. When we share our troubles with a friend they are miraculously halved, but our friend hasn't taken half of the burden. When we are celebrating, a friend will double our joy, but will not have to bring any along themselves. Friendships multiply our happiness and divide our sorrow. Friendships add something intangible but essential to our life. Without them our lives are lessened—there is something taken away that may have never even been there.

I no doubt deserved my enemies,
but I don't believe I deserved my friends.

"Song of Myself," Walt Whitman

the friends we deserve

Our enemies are small and petty and deserved. But our friends are big and grand and wonderful. Do we deserve them? They would not be our friends if we did not. They are ours and we deserve them and they deserve us. Our enemies are not chosen, not cultivated, not nurtured and encouraged. They appear by default whereas our friends are chosen and invited, nursed and encouraged. We deserve them for the work we do.

Long after you have gone, I find myself still smiling, still chuckling over something you said. I find my mood lightened, lifted, and I feel glad you came and shared some time with me. Long after you've gone, I remember you and feel warmed and comforted.

long after you've

gone

thank you

I want to thank you for being my friend. I want to sing your praises and shout to everyone how utterly brilliant you are. I want the world to know that having you as a friend has enriched my life. Without you I would flounder and lose my way, and I want you to know that I really appreciate you being my friend and that I will repay your generosity, faith, support, and kindness in the only way I know how, by being your friend in return.

Thank you.

sharing

Friendship is sharing. Not sharing our things or our money, although we may well do that as well. Friendship is sharing those moments when we feel delighted, awed, enthralled, enchanted, and overwhelmed by the beauty of nature. What is the point of seeing a beautiful sunset if you don't have a friend there to share it with? You don't have to say anything —it's all in a look.

1

sharing

2

How much better is a rainbow if you have a friend there to point it out to! And the first daffodil of spring begs to be shared, as do the bluebells, the snowdrops, and the primroses. The fall bonfires are so much richer, so much more evocative when you have a friend with you. And the crispness of the first snows of winter definitely call out for a friend to be with you to run with, to throw snowballs with, to get cold with—and after to share hot chocolate with in front of a roaring log fire.

A very good meal is best eaten with good friends. If you take a business colleague to lunch you jockey for position and talk money and ideas. If you take a lover you flirt and hold hands. If you take your children you argue and discipline. But if you take a friend you savor the food; take pleasure in the company; relax and generally enjoy everything. A meal with a friend is to be lingered over, and remembered afterward with affection.

eating with friends

my

When I was small I believed in magic. As I grew older the magic vanished and I was left alone in the harsh, real world of grown-ups. Then my friend came along and did magic for me. He brought me light and hope and comfort. He eased my burden, picked me up when I was down,

friend the magician

increased my joy a thousandfold, stayed with me when I was afraid, worked miracles around me, showed me the true meaning of unconditional love and became my magician.

a friend is like the forces of nature

When it's winter we have no evidence of the spring, yet we know it will return and bring new hope and joy. Friendship is like that. We don't have to have a set date when a friend will return; it is enough to know they are out there and will come back, bringing new hope and joy.

The forces of nature and friendship work the same, hidden at times, secret, powerful, and utterly reliable.

the value of friendship

I can make enough money to buy anything I want, and I will be lonely. I can share my life with enough lovers that I will be completely satisfied, but I will still be lonely. I can travel the world and see all the fabulous sights, and I will still be lonely. I can converse with world leaders and politicians, and still be lonely. I can cavort with film stars and celebrities, and still be lonely. I can get one phone call from a friend and feel loved, complete, not lonely any more. That's what I value the most.

When I achieve my dreams,
my goals, my ambitions I am
bursting to tell my friend.

bursting to tell

When it has all gone wrong I simply have to share my grief—but anyone will do. When life is important and the big happy stuff happens around me, I am simply bursting to tell a friend because without them it all means nothing.

My mother always straightens my collar. My partner always tucks back that bit of stray hair I have that hangs down over my forehead. My children tell me what to wear when I pick them

friends don't tidy me

up from school so I won't embarrass them. But my friends don't tidy me up—that's why they are my friends. With them I can be me and be as untidy and embarrassing as I want and they still love and accept me for being me.

up

I told you so

My friend said not to, but I did. I went ahead and did it anyway and it all went wrong. And afterwards, when I was left to pick up the pieces, my friend comforted me, and the one thing I never heard was, "I told you so."

two cups

The spring has come now
But the wind is blowing cold
I still set two cups

When will you come back
For I miss you my old friend
I still set two cups

one true friend

When things are going well for you, when you have plenty of money, your health is good and life is smiling at you, then you will have no shortage of friends. It is only when the chips are down, when life looks bleak that you learn who your real friends are.

Fairweather friends are two a penny, one true friend is worth her weight in gold.

Friendship is a vast old tree. Each friend is a leaf that has its season, its time to be, and when that time is over it will curl and fade and fall from the tree. But the space left behind is only to be filled with another leaf just the same—but different. So our friends have their seasons, their time, and when it is over, when our relationship has run its course, then they too must be allowed to fall away gracefully and naturally. There will be others. There always are.

all my friends

the field

Friendship is a field. You have to prepare it, plough it, remove the weeds, plant good seed, watch over it, water it when it needs it, scare away the birds, check the weather, and nourish it. When the time is right you will be rewarded with a great harvest. If you fail to prepare the field well your seeds will fail and the weeds will grow, at harvest time there will be nothing to gather in to fill the barns of your heart.

friendships that

cannot be broken

Friendship is an iron chain. The more links we forge, the greater the strength of that chain. But it is only as strong as each link and we must forge each well and with infinite care. The chain may become stretched, used, worn, but it cannot be broken if the friendship was pounded on anvils of love.

city of friends

I dream'd in a dream I saw a
city invincible to the attacks
of the whole of the rest of
the earth,
I dream'd that was the new
city of Friends.

"I Dream'd in a Dream,"
Walt Whitman

still remembering

Time has come and gone. Lots of water has flowed but I still remember you. Still hear your voice in my mind in times of trouble. You cannot be here now as you have gone off on new adventures, new journeys, but I still remember you as if you were here yesterday. Such is our friendship that death itself has not broken our bond, not even rippled our love. I am here and you are not, but it is as if we are still friends, still together. I am still remembering and I believe you to be so as well.

the

beauty of friendship

The true beauty of friendship is not in calling on friends in times of trouble and need, but in knowing that we might call upon them if such times arise. Friends are like savings. We don't want to squander our hard-earned money on trivialities. Savings are for emergencies which we hope will never happen. True friendship is also for emergencies which we hope will never happen. The beauty of friendships is that we can save and count our savings and hopefully never have to spend them.

the breath of kindness

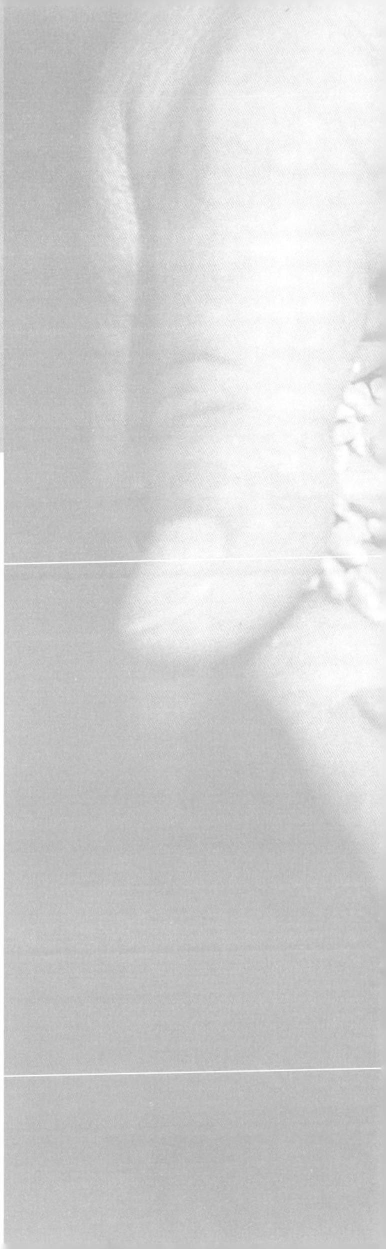

A friend is one to whom we may pour out all the contents of our heart, chaff and grain together, knowing that the gentlest of hands will take and sift it, keep what is worth keeping and with a breath of kindness blow the rest away.

Arabian Proverb

multi-talented friends

Having friends is better than having to employ counselors, psychiatrists, healers, therapists, and psychologists. Friends are multi-talented and have all the skills needed to stop you going mad. They comfort you, nurture you, help you, listen to you, give you good advice, guide you, and every day drag you back from the brink. Your friends are your medicine, your process, your cure, your doctors, and your saviors.

sharing

A friend is there, not
just for the good times,
the times of celebration
and success, but for the
dark times, the times when
things go wrong, when life
seems bleak. That is the beauty
of friendship, that we must take
the joy and the sorrow in equal
weight, and that in turn, we know
we will always have someone to
share our laughter and our pain.

If the sun is our parents welcoming us into the world with light and warmth and encouragement; and the moon is our lover, emotional, mysterious, deep, then the rainbow is the symbol of our friends. The rainbow has no purpose, it doesn't feed or clothe us, it doesn't provide us with a family or love or support—and yet what a colorless, drear world this would be without the rainbow to brighten it up. It stands as a sign that we can have joy without reason, elation without incentive and optimism without motive.

The rainbow and friendships bring us a little joy, a little comfort, a little hope.

Some flowers grow tall while others don't; some streams gush while others trickle.

differences

If we love our friends for what they are, we will have to accept their way of doing things. Not everyone shares all of our own particular attitudes. Friends are often more valuable for their differences to us than for their similarities. We must accept our friends for themselves, just as we expect them to accept us.

freedom

Friendship is a freedom

A freedom to be who we really are. To say what we really mean. To explore ourselves without guise or having to remember tact or diplomacy. Friendship is the freedom to explore human relationships without the entanglement of sex or love, and it is the freedom to make ourselves of some use without having to volunteer—we will be called upon if necessary. The freedom of friendship is in how freely it is given.

Published by MQ Publications Limited
12 The Ivories 6-8 Northampton Street London N1 2HY
Tel: 020 7359 2244 / Fax: 020 7359 1616
e-mail: mail@mqpublications.com

Text © Richard Craze 2000
Cover design: The Big Idea
Interior design: Susannah Good
Cover image: F. Cunningham, Flowers & Foliage
Interior images © Digital Vision
Series Editor: Elizabeth Carr

ISBN: 1-84072-233-9

1 3 5 7 9 0 8 6 4 2

Printed in Italy

Note on the CD

The music that accompanies this book has been specially commissioned from composer David Baird. Trained in music and drama in Wales, and on the staff of the Welsh National Opera & Drama company, David has composed many soundtracks for both the theater and radio.

The CD can be played quietly through headphones while relaxing or meditating on the text. Alternatively, lie on the floor between two speakers placed at equal distances from you. Try and center your thoughts, and allow the soundtrack to wash over you and strip away the distracting layers of the outside world.